# PRAISE FOR 1

M000190836

"In Robinson's latest action fest, Jack Sigler, King of the Chess Team--a Delta Forces unit whose gonzo members take the names of chess pieces--tackles his most harrowing mission yet. Threshold elevates Robinson to the highest tier of over-the-top action authors and it delivers beyond the expectations even of his fans. The next Chess Team adventure cannot come fast enough."-- **Booklist - Starred Review**

"In Robinson's wildly inventive third Chess Team adventure (after Instinct), the U.S. president, Tom Duncan, joins the team in mortal combat against an unlikely but irresistible gang of enemies, including "regenerating capybara, Hydras, Neander-thals, [and] giant rock monsters." ...Video game on a page? Absolutely. Fast, furious unabashed fun? You bet." -- **Publishers Weekly**

"Jeremy Robinson's *Threshold* is one hell of a thriller, wildly imaginative and diabolical, which combines ancient legends and modern science into a non-stop action ride that will keep you turning the pages until the wee hours. Relentlessly gripping from start to finish, don't turn your back on this book!" -- **Douglas Preston, New York Times bestselling author of Impact and Blasphemy**

"With *Threshold* Jeremy Robinson goes pedal to the metal into very dark territory. Fast-paced, action-packed and wonderfully creepy! Highly recommended!" -- **Jonathan Maberry, *New York Times* bestselling author of *The King of Plagues* and *Rot & Ruin***

"*Threshold* is a blisteringly original tale that blends the thriller and horror genres in a smooth and satisfying hybrid mix. With his new entry in the Jack Sigler series, Jeremy Robinson plants his feet firmly on territory blazed by David Morrell and James Rollins. The perfect blend of mysticism and monsters, both human and otherwise, make *Threshold* as groundbreaking as it is riveting." -- **Jon Land,** *New York Times* **bestselling author of** *Strong Enough to Die*

"Jeremy Robinson is the next James Rollins."-- **Chris Kuzneski, New York Times bestselling author of The Lost Throne and The Prophecy**

"Jeremy Robinson's *Threshold* sets a blistering pace from the very first page and never lets up. This globe-trotting thrill ride challenges its well-crafted heroes with ancient mysteries, fantastic creatures, and epic action sequences. For readers seeking a fun rip-roaring adventure, look no further."
 -- **Boyd Morrison, bestselling author of** *The Ark*

"Robinson artfully weaves the modern day military with ancient history like no one else."-- **Dead Robot Society**

"THRESHOLD is absolutely gripping. A truly unique story mixed in with creatures and legendary figures of mythology, technology and more fast-paced action than a Jerry Bruckheimer movie. If you want fast-paced: you got it. If you want action: you got it. If you want mystery: you got it, and if you want intrigue, well, you get the idea. In short, I $@#!$% loved this one."-- **thenovelblog.com**

"As always the Chess Team is over the top of the stratosphere, but anyone who relishes an action urban fantasy thriller that combines science and mythology will want to join them for the exhilarating Pulse pumping ride."-- **Genre Go Round Reviews**

# INSTINCT

"If you like thrillers original, unpredictable and chock-full of action, you are going to love Jeremy Robinson's Chess Team. INSTINCT riveted me to my chair." -- **Stephen Coonts, NY Times bestselling author of THE DISCIPLE and DEEP BLACK: ARCTIC GOLD**

"Robinson's slam-bang second Chess Team thriller [is a] a wildly inventive yarn that reads as well on the page as it would play on a computer screen."-- **Publisher's Weekly**

"Intense and full of riveting plot twists, it is Robinson's best book yet, and it should secure a place for the Chess Team on the A-list of thriller fans who like the over-the-top style of James Rollins and Matthew Reilly." -- **Booklist**

"Jeremy Robinson is a fresh new face in adventure writing and will make a mark in suspense for years to come." -- **David Lynn Golemon, NY Times bestselling author of LEGEND and EVENT**

"Instinct is a jungle fever of raw adrenaline that goes straight for the jugular."-- **Thomas Greanias, NY Times bestselling author of THE ATLANTIS PROPHECY and THE PROMISED WAR**

# PULSE

"Robinson's latest reads like a video game with tons of action and lots of carnage. The combination of mythology, technology, and high-octane action proves irresistible. Gruesome and nasty in a good way, this will appeal to readers of Matthew Reilly." -- **Booklist**

CALLSIGN:

# QUEEN

# JEREMY ROBINSON

## WITH DAVID WOOD

BREAKNECK MEDIA

Visit Jeremy Robinson on the World Wide Web at:
 www.jeremyrobinsononline.com

Visit David Wood on the World Wide Web at:
www.davidwoodweb.com

# FICTION BY JEREMY ROBINSON

**The Jack Sigler Thrillers**
*Threshold*
*Instinct*
*Pulse*
*Callsign: King*

**The Antarktos Saga**
*The Last Hunter - Pursuit*
*The Last Hunter – Descent*

**Writing as Jeremy Bishop**
*The Sentinel*
*Torment*

**Origins Editions (first five novels)**
*Kronos*
*Antarktos Rising*
*Beneath*
*Raising the Past*
*The Didymus Contingency*

**Short Stories**
*Insomnia*

**Humor**
*The Zombie's Way (Ike Onsoomyu)*
*The Ninja's Path (Kutyuso Deep)*

# FICTION BY DAVID WOOD

**The Dane Maddock adventures**
*Dourado*
*Cibola*
*Quest*
*Dark Entry (short story)*

**Stand-Alone works**
*Into the Woods*
*The Zombie-Driven Life*

**David Wood writing as David Debord**
*The Silver Serpent*
*Keeper of the Mists*

CALLSIGN:

QUEEN

# PROLOGUE

**Prologue
Kievan Rus'
(Present-day Ukraine)
1237**

The full moon drifted across a stormy sea of clouds, its light casting an ethereal net onto the world below. Yaroslav moved with a sense of determined purpose, pushing aside the fears bred of superstitious nonsense that threatened to overwhelm his companion.

Beside him, Kurek clutched his sword's hilt in a white-knuckled grip, every sound from the surrounding forest causing him to flinch.

"Calm yourself, Kurek." Yaroslav tried to keep the annoyance from his voice. Kurek was a good and loyal man, if not a brave one. "I assure you, there is nothing in the night that is not alive in the day."

"What about owls?" The dark-haired young man's voice trembled. "Bats are not out in the day, either."

"I said *alive* during the day. Sleeping in the daylight hours and hunting after dark does not make a creature an agent of evil." Yaroslav cast his companion a sideways glance. "You have been known to sleep during the day and engage in unsavory nocturnal activities."

The ghost of a grin played across Kurek's face, but it vanished almost as soon as it had appeared. "I like this not one bit." A rustling in the forest, far behind them, made him jump. "Do you see what I mean?" His sword was halfway out of its scabbard before Yaroslav put a reassuring hand on his arm.

"You must not let every little sound frighten you. There are plenty of creatures who have just as much right to travel at night as you do, and none of them intend us harm."

"I am not frightened." Kurek's sullen expression and dull voice made him sound ten years younger. "I am merely cautious." Reluctance evident on every inch of his face, he sheathed his sword. "I have heard stories about this place. The people who live here are…not right. They are inhospitable, never sharing a meal or offering a bed for the night. And the fishermen never venture far up the river, and never, ever travel it after dark."

Yaroslav rolled his eyes.

"We should have stayed the night in that last village," Kurek continued. "We could have eaten a hot meal and drank a cup of mead in front of a fire instead of walking through the cold and damp, being stalked by whatever is out there."

"We are not being stalked," Yaroslav said absently, his mind on the enticing picture Kurek's words had painted. He could almost taste the thick, sweet mead on his tongue. A night's rest would have been a welcome thing, but they had passed the last village at midday, and could not afford to waste daylight, not when the news he carried was so dire. Besides, they were almost out of coin, having wasted most of it on a mount that seemed hale, but proved to be a nag. Despite their best efforts to preserve her, she gave out two days later. They had sold her carcass to a farmer who wanted her for her meat and horsehide. He'd given them only a single coin and two shriveled apples in trade, but considering the man could have simply waited for them to go on their way and then butchered the nag at his leisure, Yaroslav considered himself fortunate to have gotten anything at all.

"Do you think it is true?" Kurek gazed up in trepidation at the moon as he spoke. "Do you believe the Mongols are coming again?"

"The Cumans certainly believe so." Yaroslav was thankful for the change of subject. It might distract Kurek from his fears. "Those with whom I spoke seemed genuinely concerned, and they have no reason to lie."

"Cumans!" Kurek cleared his throat and spat a wad of phlegm on the ground. The straw-haired nomads had once been known as fierce raiders, but the rise of the Mongols had led them to form peaceful relations with those they had once regarded as enemies. Many of the Rus, however, still regarded the Cumans as untrustworthy at best.

"Come now!" Yaroslav chided. "The Cumans have been peaceful for many years. They fear the Mongols as much as anyone."

"Peace!" Kurek held up his hand. "Listen," he whispered, his eyes growing wide. "Do you hear it?"

"I grow weary of this. If you are going to act like a frightened girl…"

"I am serious!" It was the intensity of Kurek's gaze more than the content of his words that brought Yaroslav up short. "Someone is following us. Whoever he is, he has been behind us for some time, and is coming closer." His eyes locked on Yaroslav's. "I am not mistaken. Listen for yourself as we walk and see if you do not agree with me."

"Very well." Yaroslav resisted the temptation to rest his hand on the pommel of his own sword. He would not let Kurek see him unsettled. It would only fuel the fear that already burned in the young man's heart. "We shall walk softly and hold our tongues. I wager it is only a lynx, or something of the sort."

They walked on in silence, careful to tread gently upon the soft earth beneath their feet. Yaroslav was just about to pronounce Kurek a fool when he heard it.

It was not the rustle of a four-legged creature rattling dead leaves as it moved through the undergrowth, but the distinctive sound of a two-legged being taking a step at a time. Kurek cast a meaningful glance at Yaroslav, but said nothing.

The sound was gone as quickly as it had come. It gave Yaroslav a chill that had little to do with the damp night air. If the sound came from a two-legged creature, it meant a man was following them—one who was taking pains to keep his approach as quiet as possible. Kurek was correct. They were being stalked.

They moved on at a steady pace, the sound growing ever closer. Yaroslav wondered who the man was and what he wanted. What if he had a bow or a crossbow? His back suddenly itched as he thought of his own vulnerability. Perhaps they should get off the path and into the shelter of the forest.

An oak tree, old and imposing, loomed up ahead. Its trunk was larger than Yaroslav and Kurek together could have spanned with their arms. Yaroslav spoke softly from the corner of his mouth.

"Do not let on that we know anything is amiss, but when we reach that oak tree, circle around behind it. I have a bad feeling." A tightening of his facial features was Kurek's sole reply, but it was enough to let Yaroslav know that his friend understood.

They did not make it to the oak tree.

Night birds set up a cry of alarm as a figure burst from the shelter of the forest. It was a man, as Yaroslav had thought, but…it wasn't.

Kurek screamed and fled into the forest on the other side of the path. Yaroslav scarcely had time to draw his sword before the thing was upon him. It was fast. Too fast to be human.

Yaroslav swung his sword, but the thing ducked beneath it

and bore him to the ground, snarling with primordial rage. Strong hands clutched his throat, the clawed tips of the beast's fingers biting deeply into his flesh. He had a brief glimpse of burning eyes, gleaming teeth and a twisted, hairy face before the world went dark.

# CHAPTER 1

## Pripyat, Ukraine

"Over here! Quickly!" The first rays of moonlight gleamed in Alexei's brown eyes and a subdued laugh underpinned his hushed whisper as he beckoned the others to follow. Oleg, his pale skin and silver-blonde hair—"piss in a snow bank," he called the color—glowing wraithlike, hurried after him. His careless footsteps quickly found one of the many potholes in the untended street, and he went down in a heap.

Hunched down in the shadow of a rusted hulk that had once been a Zhiguli, the old Eastern Bloc's version of a Fiat, Armina giggled as she watched the scene through her digital video camera. "Get up, Oleg. You're out there in the middle of the road where anyone can see you."

"I turned my ankle!" Oleg sat up, scowling at his foot as if it were somehow at fault. "Besides, there's no one around. They don't let people tour here anymore. Remember?" He began to unlace his shoe.

"Don't do that." Alexei hurried to his friend's side and hauled him to his feet. "If you've turned it badly enough, the ankle will swell and you won't be able to get your shoe on again." He hooked his arm around Oleg's waist and helped him hobble into a pool of darkness by the side of the abandoned police station.

It required a supreme effort of will for Armina to lower her camera and look around before rushing across the street to join her friends. The camera was her life, and viewed through its lens, the world held possibilities that seemed absent when seen with the naked eye.

Her fascination with video had begun innocently enough. She had posted videos online of her talking about her life and her interests. It had been such a thrill to watch her view count climb, and every "thumbs up" or positive comment, even the "*UR so hot!*" type, energized her and drove her to make and upload another video, and then another. But like with any other addiction, she always hungered for more. Hence, the web-show.

It had been the séance video that did it. She and her friends performed their own séance in an attempt to contact Anastasia, the legendary lost Romanov princess. Armina hadn't seen, heard or felt a thing, but viewer count went through the roof. Commenters swore they could see a shadow moving in the background, while others heard a whisper. Soon, the video was all over the Web, and she'd even made enough income from sponsor links to buy this new camera, which they would use to film this first-ever webisode of their paranormal investigation show.

"Where do we want to go first?" Alexei's straight, white teeth gleamed in the moon glow. "I definitely want to visit the town square."

"We're not here for sightseeing. Let's go to the stadium first. That's where the sighting was." Armina doubted the veracity of the email she had received from a viewer who claimed to have stolen into Pripyat at night and caught sight of a ghost moving through the trees inside the old stadium. She pointed the way, and they set off through the deserted husk of the once-vibrant city.

"It's safe, isn't it? The radiation, I mean?" Oleg examined his hand as if searching for signs of genetic mutation.

"Of course it is." Armina rolled her eyes, though her friends could not see it because she was once again recording them. "They've been letting people take tours through here for years. They wouldn't do it if the radiation was too high. Besides, this is not where the leak occurred."

"Close enough. Maybe it's not ghosts people have spotted here, but fallout victims! Horrible mutants that have been hiding underground all these years, just waiting to come out and feast on human flesh." Alexei elbowed Oleg, who forgot to favor his ankle long enough to chase Alexei ten meters and punch him in the shoulder.

A shiver crept down Armina's spine, like the icy breath of a nether spirit. *It's just the night air,* she told herself. The river is close by, and that makes everything cold and damp. Of course she didn't believe in ghosts any more than she believed in the power of séances, but viewers did, and the sudden closing of this ghost town a year ago, coupled with the strange rumors, made perfect fodder for a paranormal investigation. The best part was, they didn't actually need to find anything. As long as they filmed a strange shadow, an odd light or a door or gate that appeared to move under its own power, viewers would go crazy. Still, Oleg's words put her to mind of the strange stories they'd heard of late about the goings-on in Pripyat. Oleg insisted there had to be a reason the rumors had cropped up so suddenly, but who was to say? Perhaps tonight they'd find out.

They halted in the street before the hulking forms of the old family hostels. All along the buildings, silhouettes painted by graffiti artists lurked in the shadows as if waiting to spring. Armina moved out into the middle of the road and motioned for the boys to take their places. With her fingers, she made a silent countdown.

3... 2... 1...

"Greetings! I am Alexei, and this is Oleg." Alexei elbowed

the blond boy who grunted and waved. Oleg was the worst choice ever for a co-host, but perhaps he would provide comic relief. "And welcome to the first-ever episode of 'SpiritWeb,' we…" The words froze on his lips as a mournful howl cut through the night.

Armina strained to listen over the sound of her pounding heart. They all stood in expectant silence, but the sound did not come again. *A wolf*, she thought. Animals roamed the surrounding area, and sometimes wandered into the abandoned city. No reason a wolf might not be among them. They would simply have to exercise caution. She motioned for Alexei to continue.

"And that, ladies and gentlemen, is why we are here. We are paranormal investigators, and we are bringing you to a haunted ghost town. Until recently, people were allowed to tour this place, but no more. The government no longer issues permits, and has warned residents to keep away. Want to know why?"

Silence hung in the air until Alexei elbowed Oleg, who was still gazing off in the direction of the howl.

"Oh!" Oleg gave a shake like a dog drying himself, and took up the explanation. "The authorities have received reports of strange happenings here. Odd noises, like what you just heard, but also spookier, more human sounds, like people suffering. Shadowy forms leaping from building-to-building, or moving from one pool of darkness to another with superhuman speed. And we are here…" He screwed up his face. "We are here to…"

"We are here to get to the bottom of this mystery," Alexei finished. "Come along with us, as we investigate the true last frontier."

He smiled like a television news host waiting for a station break, and Armina indicated that they should investigate the sound they had just heard. Oleg paled, but Alexei, to his credit, went with it.

"Let's begin by investigating that sound."

Armina's heart was still racing as they rounded the corner past Café Olympia in search of the source of the mysterious sound. Now that the initial surprise had worn off, she was thrilled that they had something for their viewers. Likely it *was* just a wolf, but it was something, and if she knew Alexei, he would play it up to full effect.

Things went splendidly. Alexei, in hushed whispers, speculated about the source of the howling, wondering if it had been the sound of a soul in torment. He pointed out creepy, crumbling buildings, and fabricated elaborate legends about the place. He was brilliant. Oleg excelled in his own way, jumping at shadows and swiveling his head about every time they rounded a corner. Armina felt like singing. She was certain they had a hit on their hands.

Alexei was walking backward, regaling the viewers with the story of two criminals who had sought refuge in the abandoned hospital, so he was the last to see what Armina and Oleg saw. They froze, gaping at the sight. Alexei walked a few more steps, his story sputtering to a halt like a dying engine.

"What?" He frowned, clearly disappointed that his story had been interrupted. "Is something wrong with the camera?"

They were rendered mute, but Armina managed to point a trembling finger. Alexei turned and gasped at the sight. The Ferris wheel, long the most poignant and enduring image of this abandoned city, was turning.

Armina stared, mesmerized by its slow rotation, wondering if there could be any natural explanation. She racked her brain, but nothing came to mind. Wind could not move the heavy machinery, and there was little breeze tonight. It was surreal. No lights, no music. Just the slow creak of the dead attraction, come to life.

"Let's get out of here." Oleg's voice trembled and he quaked. "I want to go home."

"This is why we are here." Alexei had recovered from his moment of shock and was back in character. "Something is

happening in this place, and we are going to find out what it is."
Beckoning with theatrical aplomb, he signaled for the others to
follow him as he moved closer to the old amusement park and
its resurrected feature attraction.

Armina supposed she should at least be a little frightened,
but by returning her eye to the viewfinder, she slipped back in
to her comfort zone. The camera created a subconscious
distance between her and her subject. It was as if she was in a
richly textured virtual world where she could experience the
thrill of danger while remaining insulated from harm. Goose
flesh rose on the back of her neck as she imagined the com-
ments this video would receive once posted online. They were
going to be celebrities!

"The amusement park has been the source of many stories…AAAH!" Alexei's discourse ended in a scream of terror as
someone or something reached out of a nearby doorway and
yanked him inside. They heard him cry out once again, a
clipped sound that was immediately muffled.

And then silence.

A dark stain appeared in the crotch of Oleg's pants, and he
stood frozen in the middle of the street. His lips moved, but he
could form no words. Armina took two steps toward the
doorway where Alexei had vanished, but the fear her camera had
kept at bay now threatened to overwhelm her, and she backed
away, slowly at first, then faster.

"Oleg, we have to go get help." She sounded like a frightened child, and at this moment, she was. "You've got to come
with me. We have to get out of here now!" Oleg didn't move.
She knew she should go back, take him by the arm, and drag
him along with her, but her feet would not listen to her brain,
and they kept back-pedaling, taking her farther and farther away
from Oleg, and from Alexei, if he was still alive.

She suddenly realized she was still looking through her
camera. Even the shock of Alexei's sudden disappearance had
not been sufficient to make her stop recording. What was

wrong with her? There was no time to contemplate the question, because a dark form had just appeared from the shadow of the Ferris wheel and was headed toward Oleg with blinding speed.

She wanted to shout a warning. Even a scream would remind her immobilized body that she was still alive, still capable of movement, but as the figure came closer to Oleg, and she got her first good look at it, she could do nothing but stare in mute disbelief.

Oleg, for his part, finally overcame his paralysis, uttering a strangled cry and raising his hands in a futile attempt at self-defense. The thing, whatever it was, smashed him to the ground, clawing, biting and snarling with rage.

It was only when the monster ripped out Oleg's throat that Armina managed to lower her camera and run.

# CHAPTER 2

## The skies over Kiev, Ukraine

Queen answered her sat phone on the first ring without bothering to check the identity of the caller. She already knew who was on the other end of the line. "I suppose I'm about to learn why my flight has been diverted."

The plan had been for her to land in Siberia where she would begin her search for Rook. Queen tensed as she thought about Rook, who'd gone missing in Siberia on his last mission. She'd become close to him, closer than a teammate should, but the big lug had worked his way past her defenses and now she found herself unable to focus on much beyond locating him. If she found him alive, he'd have to answer for his silence. If she found him dead...she'd get his body home and bury him properly. His parents and sisters deserved as much. "The last time I checked, the Ukraine was not on the itinerary."

*"Sorry Queen,"* Deep Blue replied. *"If there was any other way..."* A former Army Ranger and United States President, Duncan had resigned his office, but continued to serve as Deep Blue, the guiding force behind Chess Team, a Black Ops Delta squad culled from the ranks of the Joint Special Operations

command of the United States military. The team was tasked with the defense of the nation and even the world, against the kinds of threats that most military leaders would refuse to believe even existed. Their call signs were taken from chess: Their leader, Jack Sigler, was "King." Erik Somers, a mountain of a man, was "Bishop." Shin Dae-Jung was "Knight," while Stan Tremblay answered to "Rook."

*Rook...* She felt a pinch in the back of her throat at the thought of him missing in action, possibly dead, in Siberia. She forced down the brief flicker of emotion with a shake of her head.

"I know, boss. I know." She trusted Deep Blue implicitly and while she didn't appreciate the change in plans, if the team's resident strategic guru thought there was a good reason to divert her flight, and mission, then she wasn't about to argue the point.

*"Something came up a couple of hours ago."* Deep Blue said. *"I know finding Rook is important to you. It's important to all of us. You'll be back on his trail in the morning. Scout's honor. But right now, there's a job that needs doing, and you just happen to be in the neighborhood. Make that, above the neighborhood."*

"Not anymore," Queen said as the plane hit the runway and bounced a few times before setting down. "We just touched down."

*"You do know you are supposed to turn off all electronic devices during takeoffs and landings?"*

"Right. How often do I fly commercial?" For a myriad of reasons, not the least of which was the United States' touchy political relations with Russia and the nations in her sphere of influence, it had been decided that Queen would go in quietly and keep a low profile as she conducted her investigation into Rook's disappearance. She had to admire the fact that, despite no longer being a sitting president, Deep Blue could pull enough strings to divert an international flight on a few hours notice. "On that note, you had a contact lined up for me in

Tomsk. How am I supposed to get outfitted? I couldn't exactly check my MK 23 in my cosmetics bag."

Deep Blue laughed, a rarity for him over the past several months as he dealt with the end of his presidency and began planning to get the team's new headquarters up and running. *"I've made similar arrangements in Kiev. The pickings will be slim, but I am assured your weapon of choice is in stock."*

"My weapon of choice is always with me," Queen said, looking down at her hand as she flexed it. Queen preferred to get up close and personal with her enemies. Guns came in handy, but her hands never jammed, and they were easier to clean if they got a little blood on them.

When she looked up, Queen noted the old woman sitting across the aisle peeking over the top of her enormous handbag. The woman's wide eyes bounced back and forth between Queen's hands and her face. Queen gave the woman a serious look and watched her slowly ducked down behind her bag. The woman no doubt remembered the days of the KGB and knew well enough to keep quiet about such conversations.

*"Right,"* Deep Blue said. *"In case you come across something your hands can't handle—"*

Queen fought a grin. She knew Deep Blue would never say that to her face.

*"—pick up anything you think you might need. I'll handle the tab. The proprietor will equip you and assist you with your exit strategy."*

"Will do." The plane rolled up to the gate, and confused passengers began whispered conversations, speculating about the reason for the diversion of their flight. "So tell me about this assignment."

*"We've found something at Manifold Alpha."* Hidden in the White Mountain region of New Hampshire, Manifold Alpha had once been a Manifold Genetics facility and would soon serve as the base of operations for the new and clandestine

Chess Team. *"More accurately, we've managed to decrypt one of the many memos we harvested from their network. It doesn't go into detail, but it references a project in Pripyat."*

"Shit. Are you trying to turn me into a glo-stick?" Queen stood and retrieved her bag from the overhead compartment and strode down the aisle, ignoring the resentful stares from passengers who had doubtless believed they had landed due to some sort of mechanical failure.

*"People visit there all the time. At least they did until recently. About a year ago, the government shut down all tours into Pripyat, and stopped issuing permits for individual visits. That's the only other clue we have that something is not right there."*

Queen nodded to the flight attendant who offered only a blank stare in return, and winked at the pilot, an awkward-looking man of middle years with a protuberant nose and Adam's apple to match. He'd been ogling her all the way down the aisle, and his face split into a yellow-toothed grin as she acknowledged him. She wondered how he would react if he could see the angry red skull that was branded in her forehead, a gift from General Trung, formally of the VPLA—Vietnam's elite "Death Volunteers", and now covered by a layer of makeup and a blue bandana as a concession to her need to keep a low profile.

*"I need to emphasize to you that this is a fact-finding mission. My connections in that part of the world are limited right now, and relations with Russia are tenuous at best. Not to mention, we don't know the extent of Manifold's influence there, though we would be foolish not to assume it is strong and widespread. Exercise caution."*

"Understood."

*"I'm serious. I can't send a Blackhawk to the outskirts of Kiev to rescue you without creating an international incident. Find out what's going on, if anything, and report back to me once you've gotten away safely. If Manifold is up to something in Pripyat, I'll decide how to proceed from there. Don't make yourself known, and*

*don't engage. You are to be just another shadow in the night."*

"Hooah," she said, with more force than conviction, and ended the call.

# CHAPTER 3

Queen shouldered her pack, felt at her hip for the reassuring presence of the Heckler and Koch Mark 23, though the civilian weapon was a poor substitute for her own MK 23, and slipped out of the shadows. It was well past nightfall, and no one was about. She had spent the past few hours in hiding, reading up on her destination and observing the comings and goings of disinterested local police. One pass every thirty minutes, and scarcely a glance spared for anything but the road. They were simply going through the motions.

Set atop a white pedestal shaped like an inverted triangle, block letters spelled out the name "Pripyat." Queen grimaced as she trotted past the closest thing this dead city had to a gravestone. Seen on what seemed like every website devoted to Pripyat, it had become an icon of this dead city.

Founded in 1970, the once-thriving city had been built as a home for workers at the Chernobyl Nuclear Power Plant. In its heyday, the Soviets had pointed to Pripyat as a model for the modern city, constructed according to a careful plan featuring shopping and cultural centers, modern recreation facilities, a state-of-the-art hospital and schools serving each residential area. The city had flourished for more than a decade, but it all came to an end in 1986 with the meltdown of the Chernobyl nuclear reactor. An evacuation had been hastily arranged, and citizens removed from the city thirty-six hours later, with no idea of the extent of the disaster. Most had believed they would be returning soon, and had left virtually all of their belongings behind. The city remained closed, a living time capsule memorializing the disaster. Looters and vandals had since stripped Pripyat of anything of value, but reminders lay everywhere of the people that had once called this place home.

Queen broke through a tree line surrounding the city and paused, scanning the spectral skyline, black against the moonlit sky. Abandoned buildings, now only dark husks, stood arrayed like black sentinels, keeping their silent watch. Any one of them could take an hour to search—time she did not have. One woman, one night and an entire city to cover with no clues to guide her in the right direction.

She wished the rest of Chess Team were here with her. They would scour this place in a flash and be back in time for breakfast. Thoughts of Chess Team though, led to thoughts of Rook, and that was not a road she should let her mind travel when she had a job to do.

"All right," she told herself. "Enough with the lily-ass sentimentality. Time to move."

If Manifold had a presence in Pripyat, she doubted it would be here on the outskirts of town, but somewhere deep in the heart of the dead city, perhaps near the harbor and Pripyat River. That would afford them ingress and egress without traveling surface roads. Her first target, she decided, would be the hospital. The hospital had featured cutting-edge technology for its day, and perhaps a medical facility, even an old one, might hold some appeal for Manifold. It seemed as logical a place as any to begin.

She moved with haste, slipping down pathways choked with weeds and detritus. She kept her eyes open for danger, but the city was as still as it was silent. Could Deep Blue have been mistaken? Of course, he had said it was a thin possibility, nothing more than a single mention.

She crossed Lenin Avenue and made her way up Friendship of the Nations Street, smiling that the Soviets would choose such a name at the height of the Cold War. Of course, the old Soviet Union was dead, but relations between the Americans and Russians were not much better.

A foul smell—the coppery scent of blood mixed with the stench of released bowels—made her wrinkle her nose in disgust. She knew what that meant. The smell of death was not something one ever forgot. Like a hound on the scent, she moved to where the odor was strongest, pushed aside a low-hanging branch, and grimaced at the sight that greeted her. A young man lay on his back, his limbs akimbo like a grotesque marionette. She nudged his leg and found it stiff. The blood seeping from his torn throat, however, was fresh. He had not been dead for long. She gazed down at his round face, pale skin, blonde hair and blue eyes that gave him a cherubic appearance in death. Not at all cherub-like were the red tracks that had been clawed across his fair face, the ragged red hole that had been his throat, his broken, twisted arms and his ruined torso covered in...*bite marks*? Kneeling down beside the body, she ripped open the young man's shredded t-shirt, and leaned in for a closer look. They were bite marks, all right, and although she was no medical examiner, she was sure they were human.

"What the hell happened to you, and who did it?" This was strange, but she wasn't about to waste time wondering. If her investigation didn't turn up anything else, Deep Blue could make sure the local police received an untraceable anonymous tip. Her first instinct was to cover the young man's face, but if this turned out to be a simple murder investigation for the local police, she'd already disturbed the crime scene enough. She stood and checked to make sure she'd left no muddy footprints before moving on.

When she reached the hospital, she found that, like virtually every other medical facility she'd ever seen, it was a plain, utilitarian building that looked more like a storage facility than a place where human hurts were tended.

She crouched in the brush at the edge of a large parking lot that had not yet been reclaimed by the forest. Some brave weeds had sprung up through the cracks, but the deserted lot offered no easy way to cross without being spotted. It was a good defense against intruders, but there was no way to tell if the open space had been created by design. The growth of the weeds looked natural enough. But there was only one way to find out. Queen burst from her hiding space, sprinted across the pavement and reached the hospital just seconds later.

No alarms sounded.

No traps.

No guards.

She crept along the outside wall to the double front doors. The doors were locked, but the glass was missing from both. She slipped inside, stepping carefully to avoid the shards of glass littering the floor.

The inside was worse off than the outside. She didn't know what she had expected from a place that had been abandoned for a quarter of a century, but not this. The floor was as debris-strewn as the ground outside. Dirt, leaves and bits of paper carpeted the floor, and the walls were stained by years of poor protection from the elements. She decided to begin on the top floor and work her way down. Floor by floor, she found the upper levels to be much the same. The place was a mere skeleton of what it had once been.

She was finishing her inspection of the second floor when she sensed she was no longer alone.

# CHAPTER 4

She heard it before she saw it. A low, guttural growl rose to a snarl that reverberated through the empty hall. *Maybe a wild dog wandered in here and now it thinks I've got it cornered?* Even as the thought struck her, she somehow knew that was not the case. Perhaps this dead city had her on edge, but there was something sinister, even otherworldly, about the sound.

A scuffling came from the room on her right and something leapt through the doorway coming right at her. She barely had time to move, pivoting to the side as the thing collided with her, sending her flashlight bouncing away and knocking her to the floor. The thing, whatever it was, hit the wall with a resounding crash that arrested its momentum.

Stunned, she rolled over onto her back. Her ribs burned, and the wind was knocked out of her. *That thing is stronger than Bishop.* She looked back at it in time to register a vaguely human form, and then it was crouching to spring. She reached for her Mark 23, but she was an instant too slow. It attacked.

Her fighter's instinct took over. Queen brought her knees to her chest and kicked out, catching it in midair and using its momentum to send it hurtling past her. No time to waste, she rolled over, sprang to her feet and dashed through the nearest doorway.

The room was packed with old iron bed frames. She thought to push one of them against the door, but before she could, the thing smashed through with such force that it sent her tumbling backward across the beds. Every sharp edge and broken spring seemed to tear and poke at her as she bounced once, twice, then slammed into the far corner. This time she had the presence of mind to take hold of her pistol as she flew through the air, and she came up ready to fire.

The dark, snarling shadow flew at her, and she put two silenced rounds in its chest. The snarl turned to a howl of rage and pain as the bullets tore into its body. It hit the floor and scrambled away.

She lost sight of it in the faint light, but she knew it was somewhere within this maze of iron. She heard a huff of breath and a faint scuffling on the floor, and sent a shot in that direction. The muzzle flash gave her a brief, strobe-like vision of a hairy, muscled figure coming at her from the side, teeth bared and eyes black as night.

She tried to dodge, but she was stuck in the corner with these damned beds all around. The collision was worse than any punch, kick or body slam she'd ever taken. Her head rang from the impact, and stars flashed in her eyes as she was dashed against the wall. She went limp for a moment, her Mark 23 falling from her hand. Bits of old, crumbling plaster rained down on her as her attacker rode her to the ground. She felt moist, hot breath on her neck, and nails—or claws—sank into her throat. She tucked her chin and struck the thing in the temple. It was like punching a brick wall.

Fighting with strength born of desperation, she caught it by the throat, holding it at bay just inches away from her. She drove her knee up between its legs, eliciting an angry snarl and forcing the thing to shift its weight. For all its power, it didn't seem to know anything about fighting, and was instead bent on biting and ripping her apart. Taking advantage of the momentary imbalance, she set her foot on the floor and rolled the attacking creature off her. Her left hand went to her KA-BAR knife and she stabbed blindly at where she knew her enemy to be. She felt the blade bite deeply into flesh, and this time the roar was one of sheer pain. She yanked her knife back and stabbed again, but in an instant, the beast shoved away from her and was gone. It seemed to have melted, wraithlike, into the darkness.

Knife held out in front of her, she scrambled back toward the corner, feeling around for her pistol. Her hand fell upon cool metal and she clutched it like a life preserver as a loud clang of iron on iron rang out. She caught a glimpse of one of the heavy bed frames hurtling toward her, and she rolled to the side just as it smashed to the floor with a thundering boom, landing in the spot where she had lain a split-second before. She looked up, searching for the attack she was certain would be coming any moment now.

She heard a bestial growl, the soft pad of running feet, and a shadow covered the single window for an instant before the glass shattered as the creature hurtled through the window and out into the night. Queen scrambled to her feet and climbed through the cluttered room and over to the window. She looked out in time to catch a glimpse of a hairy foot, as her attacker, whatever he or it had been, fled around a corner. *Two bullet wounds, a stab wound and a two-story fall, but the thing's not dead. What in the hell has Deep Blue gotten me into?*

One thing was for certain. She now knew what had killed the boy. Well, she didn't actually know what the thing was, but she was certain it was the cause of death. But what, exactly, was it? Even fighting it at close quarters she'd been unable to make out much about it. Its form was man-like, and just like a man, it didn't like taking a knee to the family jewels, but it seemed...*more* than human. She wished she'd gotten a good look at it. In any case, she was going to have to be extra careful. Where there was one of these creatures, there could be more.

She decided to finish her search, and if the hospital did not reveal any sign of Manifold's presence, she would next see if the thing had left a trail, perhaps blood spatter from its wounds. If the thing was a Manifold creation, it might lead her back to the place it had spawned.

She recovered her flashlight and continued her search, descending to the first floor, the basement and then the sub-basement. Pitch black and silent as a crypt, this level was a warren of mechanical rooms, their doors standing open or hanging loosely from rusted hinges. Fallen cables snaked across the dusty floor. Crumbling concrete pillars looked like they might give way at any moment. *Deep Blue, if this place comes down on top of me, I'm going to climb out of here and kick your ass.*

She made a thorough search, looking for a door, hidden or otherwise, that might lead to a secret Manifold base of operations, but she found nothing. On the positive side, nothing came leaping out of the darkness at her. *Score one for the good guys, or girls, as it were.* Only one door remained unchecked. This one, unlike the others, was closed. Holding her Mark 23 at the ready, she grasped the handle, turned it slowly, and yanked the door open.

The shrill scream practically made her hair stand on end, so high was the pitch, but she knew instantly that there was no threat here. A dark-haired teenage girl cowered on the floor. She lay on her side, her knees drawn up tight to her chest and her hands covering her face. Her jeans and t-shirt were coated in dust, and she trembled from head to toe, but she appeared otherwise unharmed.

"It's all right. I'm not going to hurt you." Queen didn't bother to keep the annoyance from her voice. She hadn't come on a rescue mission and she sure as hell wasn't here to babysit.

The girl continued to quake, crying softly into her hands, which she still held pressed to her face. Queen knelt and put a hand on her shoulder. She tried to speak to the girl in soothing tones, but it was futile. Cursing her ill luck, Queen hauled the girl to her feet, yanked her hands away, and gave her a sharp slap on the cheek—just enough to get her attention. The girl gasped and looked at her in surprise.

"You are not," she began in a quavering voice, "one of those things?" So, she not only spoke English, but had enough presence of mind to register that was the language Queen had been speaking. Queen turned the flashlight toward her own face. The girl's frozen features sagged in relief, and she fell into Queen's arms. "Thank you for rescuing for me." She stayed there for a long, dragging moment, and then her head popped up and she frowned. "But how did you know where I was? We didn't tell anyone where we were going."

"Sorry, but I didn't come for you," Queen said. "It's just dumb luck that I found you. And nobody's been rescued yet. That thing is still out there."

As though to punctuate the point, loud footsteps thumped past on the floor above. The creature was still hunting them, despite its recent injuries.

Queen bit her lip. What was she going to do with this girl? She could shove her back into the closet and come back for her later, but what if the beast found her? It had hands, so she assumed it could open a door with ease. *One problem on top of another.* "You have a name?"

"My name is Armina. My friends and I were recording our web-show when…" She shuddered, her words driven away by the memory of whatever had happened to them. "Did you find Alexei and Oleg?"

"No." Queen figured the dead body was one of the two, but this didn't seem the time to tell her new charge that. "How long have you been hiding down here?"

"I don't know. A few hours, maybe. It is so dark down here, and I am so afraid." Armina folded her arms and gave herself a squeeze, as if she could hug the fear out.

Queen looked at the girl's shaking arms and knew she

needed to get the girl settled before asking her the hard questions.

"You said you were doing a web-show?" Queen asked, feigning interest.

Armina nodded and wiped her arm across her nose. "It was supposed to be our first full length episode. We were looking for ghosts, but didn't think we'd get anything more than some sounds made by the wind, or shadows shifting from moving trees. We didn't think—we didn't know…"

"There was no way you could have known," Queen said. She could see the survivor's guilt kicking in. If the girl went down that dark road, there might not be any recovering. "How old are you, Armina?"

"Sixteen."

"And the boys?" Queen asked.

"Seventeen. Both of them."

Queen saw a familiar hardness in the girl's eyes. "Why were you really out here?"

"I told you already," Armina said, a tinge of anger seeping in. "We weren't doing drugs or fooling around."

Queen held up her hands. "That's not what I meant."

Armina looked confused.

"I meant, *who* are you escaping from? Even if you didn't know those…things were here, Pripyat isn't exactly a safe place to visit. Not only could there be gangs hiding out in the abandoned buildings but there are still radiation hotspots."

"They're well marked," Armina said, crossing her arms.

"Were you looking for signs when you ran to the hospital?"

Armina's arms dropped. Point made. "No."

Both women held their breath as footsteps passed by overhead once more. Queen waited until they faded completely before speaking again. "So, who is it?"

"My father," Armina admitted. "My mother left with another man, who didn't want me either, but I don't blame her. My father is…violent. Nearly killed her once. I try not to go home. If I do, I wait until he's asleep and try to leave before he wakes. He seems to prefer it that way, too." She shuddered. "That's why I do the web-show. When the camera is rolling, I see the world differently. It's filled with possibilities that aren't there in my ordinary life."

Armina's story struck a chord with Queen. Her childhood hadn't been too dissimilar and she'd become a violent person in her own right, though she directed it toward the right people. That Armina had found a different, more creative outlet for the hardships in her life made Queen proud of the girl. While Queen joined the military to escape her past, Armina looked through the lens of a camera and asked, "What if…"

That violence had followed the girl was a shame. She'd never be the same if they survived the night. Not without a loving family to support her. As much as Queen wanted to comfort the girl, the footsteps hadn't returned and Queen had a mission to complete.

"I'm sorry," Queen said, "but I have to ask. Did you get a look at the thing, or things?" Queen pressed her. "Do you have any idea what they are?"

Armina looked her in the eye and nodded. Slowly, she bent down and picked up something up off the floor. She held it out to Queen, who saw that it was a digital recorder.

She flipped it on and switched it to playback mode. The faces of two laughing boys appeared on the screen. The one on the right, the one they called Oleg, was definitely the one she had found lying dead on the side of the road.

"Here, let me." Armina took the camera from her, scanned forward, and handed it back.

Queen watched as Alexei disappeared from sight, and then as something hurtled out of the darkness, coming right at Oleg. As a shaft of moonlight fell upon its dark form, Armina hit the pause button.

Queen did not permit surprise to register on her face. In fact, there was not much in this world that surprised her anymore. The creature was, as she had thought, humanlike. Its face was in shadow, but she could clearly make out its powerful frame coated in fine hair. One hand was upraised, the light glinting off short claws. Not for the first time in her life, she found herself staring at something out of legend.

"It is the oborot." Armina's whisper was soft, almost reverent.

"The what?" Queen cocked her head.

"I think you would call it," the girl said, her voice quavering, "a werewolf."

# CHAPTER 5

"A werewolf." Saying the word aloud somehow gave substance to the mythical creature, making it seem a little less surreal in Queen's mind. Someone who had not seen and experienced the things Chess Team had faced might have scoffed, but not her. "All right, then. I don't have any silver bullets, but I've got a few tricks up my sleeve." Time and supplies had been short, and Deep Blue had been correct when he said his connection had limited resources at her immediate disposal, but she had a couple of surprises in her backpack in case she should need them. "Okay Armina, let's get you out of here."

It grated on her not to see the mission through, but Deep Blue had made it clear that she was to slip in and out quietly. Besides, she now had Armina to deal with, and she wasn't going to let the girl get torn apart like Oleg. She'd get the girl to safety and report in.

She returned the camera to Armina and led the girl back up the stairs. When they reached the first floor, she turned off and pocketed her flashlight. Letting her eyes adjust to the moonlit shades of gray all around her, she thought about the situation here. What *would* she tell Deep Blue? That she had reason to believe Manifold was manufacturing werewolves in

Pripyat? That wasn't anywhere near good enough. At the very least, she needed to confirm beyond a shadow of a doubt that Manifold was here, and locate their base of operations. Without that information, there would be no possibility of a surgical strike under the noses of the Russians. Anyone they sent in would be going in just as blind as she was. Like it or not, she wasn't finished yet.

"Armina, we need to find a safe place for you to hide." The girl frowned and began to protest, but Queen put a finger over her lips. "I promise I won't leave you. I have more work to do here, and I have to be out before sunrise, but I swear I'll take you with me."

"Don't just leave me here. Maybe I can help you." Armina's words were brave, but her voice was a frightened whisper.

"I don't think so. I don't have time to explain, but I am in a dangerous line of work, and I believe there are some people here who are just as dangerous, if not more so, than the oborot."

"What people are you talking about? Where are they? We didn't see anyone out there, except…"

"What?" Queen's pulse raced. If Armina could give her a clue to the whereabouts of Manifold, that would put her one step closer to success. "Did you see something?"

"I was just thinking about the moment before the oborot came after Oleg." She shivered and her face fell. "Alexei was not attacked. He just disappeared, as if someone grabbed him. Could it have been those people?"

"I don't know," Queen admitted. "Let's have another look at your video. Back up to the part where Alexei was taken." Armina complied, and they watched as the boy was there one moment and gone the next. "Back up and play it again," Queen said. "Can you slow it down?" Armina nodded, and the scene unfolded again in slow-motion. "Freeze it there!" Armina paused the video. "Good! Now zoom in on Alexei."

Armina complied. As the image expanded on the screen,

her eyes widened and she tapped the image. A gloved hand was wrapped around Alexei's wrist. "I was right! Someone did take Alexei."

"Definitely. I don't know for sure how it fits together, but it's worth investigating. I see this was over near the amusement park." Queen froze. Something strange about the video had just registered with her. It was so obvious that she had to laugh. So intent was her focus, first on Oleg and the oborot, and then on Alexei, that she had ignored the other oddity.

"What's wrong?" Armina looked all around, as if Queen had spotted some danger.

"Nothing. Hit play for me." This time, her eyes were not on the boys, but on the Ferris wheel in the background. It was turning. "When you were out there, did you see the Ferris wheel turning?"

"Yes, we did. You missed that part when I forwarded it to the attack, but we noticed it right away. We were going for a closer look when all the rest happened." Armina winced as if the very words pained her. "I have heard that Pripyat is haunted and I never believed it. But abandoned rides that start up on their own, and oborots roaming the streets? It must be true."

"I don't think Pripyat is haunted." Queen grimaced. If her instincts were correct, Manifold had set up operations some-where in the vicinity of the old amusement park, and as an added security measure, they had run a line to the old Ferris wheel and put it in working order again. Turn it on when the occasional stranger sneaked into the park, and the person would hopefully run away in fright, telling everyone the place was haunted. Get enough people spreading the ridiculous tale of a haunted amusement park, and you've got a surrounding community of skeptics ready to dismiss the story of an oborot, should one ever get out. And she had no doubt that this oborot, werewolf or not, was a product of one of Manifold's twisted experiments. She gave the girl's shoulder a squeeze. "Now, let's figure out where to hide you, and I'll be off."

"No!" Armina didn't sound frightened, but determined. "I will be safer with you. You have a gun. Besides, I can take you right to the amusement park. It will be faster for you."

"But what will I do with you when we get there?" Queen couldn't believe she was even considering this. It was ridiculous. She couldn't have the kid slowing her down. Then again, if the girl could quickly guide her to the amusement park, that *would* be a great help.

Armina screwed up her face in concentration. "There are some old soft drink machines nearby. They're empty. Close me up in one of those until you can come for me." She saw the hesitation in Queen's eyes. "If you don't take me, I'll just follow along behind you."

"Try that, little girl, and I'll truss you up and hang you from the ceiling like a wind chime. You got me?"

"I'll scream." Tears welled in her eyes, but the resolve there was evident. "Or I'll make whatever noise I can and the oborot will get me anyway. Just let me go with you. I don't want to be here alone anymore."

For a brief instant, Queen considered hauling the girl back to the basement and sticking her, bound and gagged, into the closet where she'd found her. Of course, then Armina would have no way of running if the oborot should return. Besides, Queen already knew she was not going to leave the girl behind. When she looked into Armina's eyes, she was taken back to a time when she had not been Queen, but simply Zelda—a frightened, mistreated girl who survived by keeping the tiniest spark of determination burning inside the walls she erected between herself and the outside world. Armina had a little spark of that same determination enshrouded in a fog of fear and Queen would not extinguish that flame for anything in the world.

"All right. You can come along, but you keep up and keep quiet. Understand?" Beaming, Armina nodded. Queen looked her up and down. Her black jeans would do fine, but the bright yellow tank top and pale skin would make her stand out too much in the darkness. "We need to make a couple of changes. Put this on." Queen unzipped her black jacket and handed it to Armina. While the girl slipped it on, Queen, now in clad only in black pants and a black t-shirt, set about rubbing dirt over her well-defined arms. She rubbed a little on her face for good measure and instructed Armina to do the same.

"I think our furry friend is gone, but stay close to me," she instructed as they completed their preparations. "We're going to keep to the shadows as much as possible. And if I tell you to do something, you do it immediately, with no questions asked."

"All right." Armina cocked her head and gave Queen a thoughtful look. "You know, you never told me your name."

"My name doesn't matter." She immediately saw the hurt in Armina's eyes and amended her statement. "It's Zelda, but nobody calls me that." She knew giving her real name was a breach of protocol, but since Chess Team became a black-op, she officially no longer existed. Knowing her first name wouldn't help identify her anymore than knowing her call sign.

"You're pretty," Armina said. "I didn't notice until we got into the light." She pointed to the blue bandana covering Queen's hair and forehead. "But you shouldn't cover your hair."

Queen rolled her eyes and turned her head away. Beauty wasn't something she thought about much since the branding. She didn't go in for that girly crap anyway, but she tried to piece together a compliment that would help soothe Armina's mind. "Never wish for what someone else has. You're a good looking kid. You'll be a beautiful woman—a princess."

"A princess." Armina smiled. "I like that. We can be the queen and princess escaping from the lair of the evil wizard who wants me to marry him."

Queen smirked. What were the chances she'd have come up with 'Queen' on her own? "Come on then, princess. Let's make our escape."

# CHAPTER 6

"Sir, we've got movement in the area of the stadium." Andrew kept his eyes glued to the monitor as he spoke. "Moving fast, too."

"Is it our escaped subject?" Darius leaned down for a closer look. He was still perturbed at the carelessness of his staff. A bare-bones operation they might be, but there was no excuse for what had happened. If the escapee should make its way to civilization before regression, there was no telling what might happen. This was not the first escape, either, and still no one had discovered how the subjects were getting out. And if Manifold were to find out about it, well, Darius already had one strike against him.

"It's difficult to say, but we appear to have two distinct heat signatures." Andrew sighed. "We need better equipment. Our security system covers such a limited area, and we have so few cameras. If we had more…"

"You have what Manifold deems you need." Darius's rebuke cracked like a whip, bringing the man into line. "Need I remind you we are hiding in plain sight here? Cameras and sensors will be noticed unless they are hidden perfectly. That is why we are so limited in that area. If you feel yourself incapable of performing the duties of your position, that is another conversation entirely. Is that something you wish to discuss?"

"No sir." Andrew's face reddened. "If they continue on their present course, they should pass the fixed camera at the stadium. Should I send the squad out to snatch them?"

"Not just yet. We've already added one subject to our pool tonight. Keep an eye on them and see what they are doing. Worst case, we send one of the men out in a police uniform to warn them off for trespassing. No need to make things any more complicated than necessary." He grimaced. Snatching the boy had been a risk, but they were in sore need of fresh subjects. The progression was still not working as it should, and regression wore on the body. Each cycle left the subject a little weaker, and a little less human.

"They're about to pass by the camera now." Andrew seemed to have already forgotten the earlier chastisement. He was young and a bit inept at anything that did not involve a computer, but he was eager, hungry for advancement and had no moral issues whatsoever with the work they did here. "It's two women. Rather, a woman and a girl. Wait! That's the girl who was at the amusement park earlier. The one whose friend we snatched."

"You're missing the important detail, Andrew." The young man was correct about the girl, but Darius had eyes only for the woman. She was a trim, athletic little blonde, and attractive, if a touch on the muscular side, though the night surveillance camera did not offer the best resolution. She wore black pants, t-shirt, and a backpack, but what interested Darius was the gun she held in her right hand. He tapped the image on the screen. "Why is she armed?"

"Sorry. Let me see what I can do." With a few clicks, Andrew zoomed in on the woman's face, took a set of screen captures, and fed them into Manifold's security system. They waited for the system to come up with potential matches. The quality of the images would present a challenge, but the facial recognition system was state-of-the art. If this woman was known to Manifold, they'd have her identity in a matter of minutes.

When the search result turned up onscreen, it gave Darius pause. This was a surprise, and not a pleasant one.

"Zelda Baker, aka: Queen," Andrew read. "Kill on sight. That's it." He turned to Darius, a deep frown on his face. "If Manifold knows about this woman, there should be more on her. Much more than what they're giving us. There's no bio, no psychological, no analysis. Why would this be all they give us? Is she that unimportant?"

"Quite the opposite," Darius said. "It means she's too important for the likes of you to have access to information about her. Don't feel badly about it. You'll get there one day."

"So what do I do now?" The enthusiasm had drained from Andrew's voice, and its dull tone matched his stony expression.

"You see what it says there. Send the squad out to take care of them." That raised Andrew's spirits a little. He tapped the intercom and smiled as he passed along the Kill on Sight order.

Darius left and headed back to his office. His level of clearance was higher than Andrew's, though it was lower than it had been once upon a time. Perhaps he could learn a little bit more about Zelda Baker. If not, that meant she was a prize, and he just might earn his way back into Richard Ridley's good graces by killing her himself—that is, if they ever heard from Ridley again. His last contact was a blast to all Manifold facilities, requiring them to continue research, but go silent and remain so until he made contact again. And if Ridley made contact before their research bore fruit, at least he'd have Queen to present as a sacrificial lamb.

# CHAPTER 7

Something moved up ahead in the midst of the undergrowth surrounding the stadium. Suppressing her instinct to attack first and ask questions later, Queen grabbed Armina by the shoulder and shoved her to the ground. A man clad all in black and armed with a Kalashnikov AK-74, knelt behind a bush, clearly on the lookout. She could easily slip past the man, but she doubted Armina would be able to do the same. Furthermore, he was unlikely to be the only one out searching for her. She'd have to find a quiet way to take care of this.

She mouthed the words "stay put" to Armina. The girl nodded, fear gleaming in her eyes. Unsheathing her KA-BAR, Queen made her move.

She had plenty of practice moving silently through any terrain. Plus, there was a faint breeze that rustled the leaves, covering any sound she might make. She made a slow, methodical circle, all the while worried that the man, or one of his cronies, would spot Armina. Her pulse quickened as she crept closer to her target. The last ten feet was clear of any trees or ground cover. It seemed a yawning chasm. If she wanted to shoot him, she could take him out from here with ease, but the suppressor on her Mark 23 would not eliminate all sound, and that would risk bringing more Manifold men down on her position. Besides, she wanted some answers.

She rose up on the balls of her feet, ready to spring at a moment's notice, and crept across the intervening space as silently as a cloud passing over the face of the moon. The man never knew she was there. At least, not until she delivered a roundhouse kick to his temple that knocked him stupid. He slumped over on his side, his rifle falling to the ground. Queen was on him in an instant, pinning him down, her knife at his throat and a gloved hand over his mouth. She had made certain to kick him hard enough to stun him but not hard enough to kill him.

"Are you working for Manifold Genetics?" she whispered. The man blinked, his eyes a bit foggy, and then he nodded. "Are you experimenting on people here?" The man shrugged. "You're lying." She pressed down on the knife.

His head was rapidly clearing, and as his eyes focused in on Queen, surprise and fear melted away, replaced by contempt. It had happened far too many times—her size and looks invited underestimation, especially from stupid people, who seemed to comprise the vast majority of the world's population. This man appeared to be one of those, and she could sense he was about to make a big mistake.

"Last chance to live, pal. Tell me what Manifold is up to here." Her voice was a whisper of frozen velvet, but he could not sense the danger that lurked there. He stared up at her, his eyes flinty with defiance, and gave a little shake of his head.

"Fine by me. One less asshole in the world."

His eyes suddenly grew wide and he gave a vigorous nod. *What a pansy.*

"I'm going to move my hand and let you answer me. Keep it quiet or that's it for you. Do you understand?" He nodded again, and she slid her hand up to his nose in case she had to clamp it quickly back over his mouth.

"You can rot in hell!" He grabbed her knife arm with his

left hand and reached for her throat with his right.

Any member of Chess Team could have told this idiot that Queen, despite her size, was no weak little girl to be tossed around like a rag doll. Queen batted his grasping hand away from her throat as easily as swatting a fly, covered his mouth before he could cry out any more, and forced her knife down toward his throat.

The man now clutched her knife arm in both hands, trying desperately to keep the razor sharp KA-BAR at bay. He was strong, but not strong enough. Sweat beaded on his forehead and terror filled his eyes as the blade of her knife came down in slow motion like a guillotine in sore need of WD 40. He thrashed about, trying to dislodge her, but he could not. As Queen looked into his eyes, every horror perpetrated by Manifold flashed through her mind. This man, she reminded herself, was another agent of their evil, and an accomplice in the sacrifice of humanity for the sake of Richard Ridley's lust for power. With a grunt, she forced her knife down. Warm blood sprayed her hand as the KA-BAR did its work with cold efficiency.

Something buzzed past her head and she heard the report of a rifle. She hit the ground and rolled to cover, trying to pinpoint the direction of the shooter. Another bullet buzzed past her, and she knew the shooter was somewhere behind Armina. The girl had not cried out. Either she was being exceptionally brave, or they had taken or perhaps killed her.

"Armina!" she called out as loudly as she dared. "Can you hear me?"

"Yes." The girl's voice was faint. "What is happening? Where are you?"

"Crawl to the sound of my voice. Hurry!" To her credit, Armina ceased her questions and complied immediately. Moments later she emerged from the underbrush, her face pallid but her eyes resolute. "We're going to make for the stands." Keeping low, she led Armina toward the old stadium that overlooked the grounds through which they now crept. It was difficult to imagine this sparsely wooded area had once been an athletic field. *Good thing it's no longer an open field,* she thought, or *we'd be dead.*

Just short of the stadium, the wooded area gave way to a wide swath of cracked asphalt that had once been a track. Queen looked around for pursuers and, seeing none, grabbed Armina by the arm, took a deep breath and dashed across the open space.

They had almost made it across when someone opened fire on them.

A torrent of bullets tore into the stadium's foundation, sending up a spray of concrete that stung as it scoured Queen's face. No slugs ricocheted their way though, and they scrambled up the steps and behind the shelter of a low concrete wall that ran in front of the bottom row of seating. The stadium itself remained in surprisingly good condition after all these years. Its foundation appeared solid and the rows of wooden bleachers were still in place, though the wood was decaying in places. It looked to Queen as if, at any moment, spectators would come filing through the concourses and take their seats. *This is what they mean by 'ghost town,'* she thought. *It truly feels like a place frozen in time.*

"You see that concourse up there?" She inclined her head to the exit tunnel several rows up. Armina nodded. "When I start shooting, you make for that tunnel as fast as you can. When you get on the other side, find a place to hide and I'll catch up."

Queen knew their enemies would be keeping a close eye on the spot where they had last seen her and Armina, so she crawled forty feet along the wall before popping up, weapon in hand, looking for a target.

A dark-clad man carrying a rifle was creeping across the track. Queen spared a moment to take careful aim and squeezed off two rounds. The man went down, but her attack was immediately answered by gunfire from over her left shoulder. She ducked down behind the protection of the wall and blindly fired off three shots in the attacker's direction. She hoped that would buy Armina enough time to get away. She stole a glance toward Armina and was relieved to see her disappear into the tunnel. She turned back in time to see a muzzle flash in the distance as the Manifold agent took a potshot at the heels of the fleeing girl. The distance was too far and the cover too dense for an accurate shot with a handgun, so Queen held her fire, but now she had a bead on him.

The agent probably expected Queen to escape by the same path as Armina. He would be wrong. Remaining down and protected, she crawled along the bottom row of seats, picking her way through debris and trying to make as little sound as possible. She moved past the spot from which the last shot had come and crawled to the stairs on the opposite end. If the man had half a brain, he'd soon be growing suspicious that she had not yet tried to escape. She would have to do this fast.

She crept down the stairwell and peeked up over the railing. There he was, slinking through the darkness, careful to always keep a tree between himself and the spot where Queen had last fired. She picked up a chunk of concrete and flung it down to the far end of the stadium, where it bounced twice on the bleachers, the decaying wood muffling the sharp cracking sound before it clattered down the concrete steps.

Unable to see much in the darkness, the man open fired in the direction of the noise. Bullets sparked off the metal framework that supported the bleachers, and rotten wood splinters erupted like a geyser. The sound of her approach masked by the barrage of gunfire, Queen sprinted across the track and took him from behind. She buried her knife at the base of his skull.

Her victory was short-lived. She heard the thud of several booted feet coming her direction. With no time to spare, she grabbed the dead man's Kalashnikov and dashed away.

Armina called to her as soon as Queen burst through the

concourse. "Zelda, I'm over here!"

"Don't use my name," Queen muttered, as Armina beckoned from the blackness of a tunnel that led back underneath the stadium. "I can't protect you and take care of business at the same time. You get back inside there and hide. I'll make sure they follow me and not you."

"But I can't see anything back there. It's pitch black."

"Even better. They won't be able to see you." Armina had held it together surprisingly well up to this point, but now her lip trembled and Queen feared the girl would soon lose it. "Calm down. Look, I'll come with you. Let's go." She shoved the girl back down the tunnel and flicked on her flashlight long enough to see sagging metal doors twenty feet back. They hurried down the tunnel and squeezed inside, leaving the doors ajar just as they had been.

They found themselves in a locker room. A bench ran down the center, and cage-like metal lockers, large enough for a person to stand inside, lined the walls on either side. An open doorway on the far end led to a shower room.

The clatter of footsteps echoed outside, and Queen heard muffled voices. *They aren't very good at keeping quiet, are they?* She chalked it up to the dual arrogance of superior numbers and testosterone. In any case, she had no time to waste.

"Get inside one of these lockers and don't make a sound until I come back for you." She pushed Armina into the closest locker and hastily pushed the door partway closed. She hurried to the locker room doors, taking off her backpack as she ran. She peered through the open door to see the silhouettes of at least five men coming slowly down the passageway. Perfect!

She took out an F1 fragmentation grenade, nicknamed "limonka," or "little lemon," yanked the pin and released the spoon. Giving it a second to cook, she pitched it through the open doorway and dashed back into the locker room, praying she didn't trip over or slam into anything in the darkness. The F1 had a four and-a-half second fuse, and the men in the tunnel had no time to react before it blew.

The sound was deafening, and the light from the flash gave Queen a quick glimpse of the shower room up ahead. She ducked inside and readied the Kalashnikov. She doubted she'd gotten lucky enough to take them all out, and she was proved correct when a flash of gunfire erupted from the far end of the locker room by the doorway. The guy was shooting blind, and the bullets spattered the wall outside the shower room. She responded with a quick burst of gunfire and then rolled to the side as a hail of bullets buzzed past her like angry hornets. She had given away her position, but that was by design. She wanted to draw them past Armina's hiding place, and get them to pursue her instead.

She looked around for an avenue of escape, knowing she'd better find one quickly or she was royally screwed. She could just make out the faint outline of rusted showerheads lining the far wall, and hooks for towels along one side. She saw nothing.

And then it struck her. She could see! So where was the light coming from? The grenade and muzzle flashes had temporarily blinded her night vision, but now that she was adjusting to the darkness, she could make out a small window, just above eye level, set in the center of the exterior wall. Rusted blinds hung across it, filtering in the tiniest glimmer of moonlight. It would be a tight squeeze, but she could make it. She opened up with the Kalashnikov, blowing every shard of glass out of the frame. She heard shouted instructions in the locker room, and knew the Manifold men believed themselves to be under attack.

"Armina," she whispered loudly, "Stay where you are, and behind cover no matter what happens or what I say next. In fact, cover your ears."

A whispered, "Okay," was Armina's only reply.

Queen shouted, "Hurry, go out the window," hoping the men pursuing her would assume Armina escaped first. Another burst of gunfire replied to her voice as she dashed to the window and hauled herself up and out. "Go ahead, I'm hit" she shouted, doing her best to sound wounded. She waited there outside the window, readying another F1 and listening to the sound of pursuit as the remaining Manifold men dashed into the shower room after her. *They really don't learn, do they?* She pitched the grenade through the window and relished the shouts of surprise and subsequent explosion. If Armina had stayed hidden in her locker outside the shower room, she'd be fine, but Queen couldn't help worrying about the girl as she ran into the night.

# CHAPTER 8

"What report do you have from the security force?" Darius's palms were sweaty and his pulse throbbed in his temple. He had been correct about Zelda Baker, or "Queen," as she was known. She was no ordinary operative. Though there remained a wealth of information on her that he was not permitted to access, he had learned enough to be gravely concerned that they had drawn the attention of such a dangerous enemy. The sole consolation was that she appeared to be alone rather than accompanied by her entire squad.

"Nothing in a while." Andrew's voice was tight. "The last report I had was that we'd lost two men, but they had cornered her in a locker room in the stadium. No one has reported back since." He turned and fixed Darius with a nervous look. "I don't know what to do now."

"We have to assume she's eliminated the security squad, and will soon be coming this way. Continue trying to reach the men in case any are still alive." Darius ran a hand across his bald pate, feeling the ridges created by old scars. "If she reaches the amusement park…" He paused, relishing the expectant smile on Andrew's face, "Perhaps we shall have the opportunity to play with a few of our toys."

**Queen vaulted** a concrete barrier and turned back to watch the concourse. She hated leaving Armina alone, even for a short while, but she had to make sure she'd eliminated the Manifold force before going back inside. If any of them remained alive, they should soon be coming out after her. Cautiously, of course, but they would come. Eyes and rifle trained on the locker room entrance, she counted the seconds in her head.

One minute…

Two minutes…

Three minutes…

That was long enough. Finger on the trigger, she hugged the wall as she made her way back to the locker room. That last grenade must have finished them. If any of the men remained alive, surely they would have come out by now. She rounded the corner and entered the tunnel just as a black-clad man stepped through the doorway.

He was quick, but she was faster. She put a single round in his gut—the only round left in the Kalshnikov, but it did the job. He fell hard against one of the doors and slid to the ground, leaving a smear of blood behind him. His own rifle fell from his hands, forgotten as he pressed his hands over the wound, seeking in vain to hold the life in. Like so many men before him, he'd believed himself immortal. Queen could tell it from the shocked disbelief in his eyes, but he'd get no sympathy from her. She drew her Mark 23 and took aim.

He looked up at her, saw his death reflected in her eyes, and grinned. "You're too late. Your girl is dead." Malice dripped from every word.

"You're lying." She suddenly felt numb. It couldn't be true.

"Zelda! Is that you?" he mimicked. "She took a bullet on the ricochet. It might even have been you who did it to her. Who knows? I finished her off for you, so the way I see it, you owe me a quick death like the one I gave her."

"Liar!" Queen hissed. She drew her knife, determined to make his last moments on earth the most agonizing time of his life.

"I even got a souvenir." His voice was now raspy, almost a death rattle. He only had seconds left. He held up a digital video camera. Queen recognized it immediately.

She roared like a feral beast, all her rage and frustration boiling over. Forsaking both of her weapons, she kicked the man square in his grinning mouth. Teeth shattered and blood sprayed his face. She kicked again and felt the satisfying crunch of breaking bone. She spun, putting all her power into the kick, and drove her heel into his temple. His neck snapped, and his head lolled to the side, the grotesque remnants of his last wicked grin lingering on his face.

She dashed into the locker room, still clinging to an irrational hope that the man had lied to her, but deep down, she knew it was not so. When the beam of her flashlight fell on Armina's slumped figure, Queen's throat tightened and her vision clouded. *No!* She would not cry! She had known pain all her life, and seen enough death for a hundred lifetimes. She would not let this break her.

She knelt down and drew Armina close to her. "I should have protected you," she whispered. "You deserved better than this." Dark memories of her own teen years came unbidden to her mind. She thought of her alcoholic father, her mother's tragic passing and years of feeling like an outcast and an oddity. Miseries that led her down some dark paths before she found her way again. Life should not be that way. Children should be kept safe from the darkness of the real world. Armina had been almost a young woman, true, but she was still innocent.

Queen kissed the girl on the top of her head and laid her back down. She would ask Deep Blue to make sure Armina's body was returned to her family, as well as Oleg's to his family. Right now, though, she had unfinished business. She shined her light down on Armina, taking a long look at this innocent victim of Manifold's wickedness. She let the anger wash over her, soaking her to the bone with righteous rage. She would see to it that this evil was punished.

She returned to the dead man and gave his body a quick search. He had nothing useful on him—his Kalshnikov was empty and any reloads he might have carried must have already been expended. He bore neither a knife nor a handgun. She was about to leave him when something caught her eye—a tiny headset. She slipped it off and held it up to her own ear. She heard nothing at first, but then someone spoke.

*"Sweeper squad, do you copy? Anyone copy?"*

"I copy," Queen growled, pouring into her words every bit of anger and hatred she could muster.

*"Who is this?"* Surprise rang in every syllable.

She yanked off her bandana and used it to rub away the makeup concealing her bright red skull and star brand. Meant to scar her physically and emotionally, the brand had instead become a reminder of her strength—of what she could overcome. She embraced the symbol of the Death Volunteers and made it her own. "The Angel of Death," she said. "And I'm coming for you."

# CHAPTER 9

Queen knew she was being much more reckless than she ought to, but they already knew she was here and, likely as not, they would be taking up defensive positions, hanging back and waiting for her. It had been impulsive to announce her presence and her intentions that way, but she wanted blood. Deep Blue could feel free to be as pissed off as he liked, but for her, this was no longer an intelligence-gathering mission.

The Ferris wheel, the amusement park's most prominent feature, loomed up ahead, a dark silhouette in the moonlight. Everything around her was as silent as death.

"Where are you?" she whispered. She hoped her hunch about the amusement park was correct, and it would lead her to Manifold's headquarters. She passed a dilapidated booth where jagged chunks of broken glass gleamed like fangs in the window casing. A graffiti artist had painted a sinister, yellow eye on the side of the booth below the window. She knew the Pripyat Funfair had never actually opened to the public, the Chernobyl disaster having forced the city to evacuate prior to its scheduled first day of operations. She wondered if excited children had watched its construction, just waiting for the moment they could walk up to this booth and buy their tickets for the rides—

children who had no idea that death loomed just over the horizon. Kids like Armina, who never had cause to contemplate their mortality. She felt an ache deep within her soul. When had she gone so soft? How could a girl she scarcely knew have worked her way into Queen's heart in so short a time? Maybe it was her worry over Rook that was twisting her insides.

*Rook.*

No, she was not going to think about that right now. She'd lose her focus, and that could mean death.

A predatorial growl saved her.

She didn't see the oborot that made a mad dash for her, but its throaty sound of hunger snapped her thoughts back to the present just in time for her to pivot out of its way as it grabbed at her. As she sprang to the side, she grabbed the creature by the back of the neck and forced its throat down onto a triangle of broken glass twice the size of her hands. The oborot made wet, gurgling gasps as its life's blood poured from its body, oozing down the side of the booth and covering the yellow eye in a red veil. It made a few feeble swipes at Queen, each weaker than the one before, until finally it went limp. The shard of glass snapped under its dead weight, and the oborot slid face-first to the ground.

Queen used her foot to roll the oborot over onto its back. She could tell by the other wounds it had sustained that it was the same creature she'd fought earlier. No wonder it had died so easily. It had probably been on its last legs when it came after her, but unable to resist its hunger or lust for killing—whatever it was that drove the beast. She couldn't spare time to examine it closely, but it was much less animal-like than she had expected. It was a muscular man. His face, neck and forearms were covered in hair, but the hair was not coarse like typical body hair, but fine. Its fingernails were long and thick. Otherwise, she saw little else to distinguish it from an ordinary human being.

"What's your story?" she whispered. *Did you sign up for this duty, or are you another one of Manifold's victims? Are there many more like you?* She hoped not, but she had a feeling her one-woman war would only get more difficult from here.

She scanned the amusement park, trying to decide where to begin. To her left was a broken down boat-swing ride, the ship in which riders sat lying on its side. Up ahead lay an old bumper car ride. Patches of moss and weeds grew all over the old track, and a couple of upended cars were scattered about, while others sat, as if waiting for the ghosts of Pripyat to hop in and go for a spin. It looked to Queen like the bedroom of a child who hadn't picked up his toys in a long time. The roof, if there had ever been one, was gone, leaving only the metal framework that provided electricity to the cars.

In the middle of the track she spotted a trap door. She hurried to the bumper car ride, vaulted the side railing, and made for the door.

She had only taken three steps when she heard a gentle whirring sound, and the closest bumper car shot toward her. She leapt out of its way, but it caught her heel and sent her stumbling forward. Before she could recover her balance, another car careened into her. She rolled up over its hood and fell heavily onto her side, blood filling her mouth as she bit her tongue. *Damn!* Was someone controlling these cars?

Both cars had turned around and were coming at her again, bouncing over the uneven track. She took off at a dead sprint, easily outdistancing them. Another bumper car came in from the side, almost upending her, but she was ready, and leaped over it. As she hit the ground, she heard a satisfying crash as the three cars collided.

Reaching the trapdoor, she hauled it up and tossed it to the side, aware that the bumper cars were coming for her again. She shined her flashlight down into the hole and was disappointed to see that it was merely a small mechanical room no more than six feet across with no doors or trapdoors inside that could take her any farther. *Scratch that off the list.*

She had no time to ruminate on it, because the bumper cars were almost on top of her again. She made straight for them and leaped onto the hood of the center car. The moment her foot touched down she jumped again, leaping past the moving car. Falling forward, she rolled, though her backpack made it more of an awkward tumble.

*"Impressive,"* a voice said as she came to her feet. For a moment, she thought she had left the Manifold agent's head-phone on, but then she realized the voice was coming from all around her. Nor was this the voice of the person she'd heard speaking through the earphone. This man had a deep, smoky voice brimming with arrogance. *"You shouldn't have come here, Queen."*

Lighting flashed all around, or so it seemed, but Queen quickly realized they were strobe lights set each corner. Disoriented by the flickering, she turned and ran for the nearest side rail. The world seemed to move in slow motion, a black and white slideshow played out before her eyes. Another car shot toward her and she couldn't avoid this one in time. Pain lanced through her legs as the car smashed into her shins. She fell face-first onto the hood, her breath leaving her in a *whoosh*. Wincing, she pulled herself up, thinking to climb inside.

The car cut sharply to the left and screeched to a halt, sending her tumbling to the ground. *"You had no idea what you'd find here, did you? No...you wouldn't have come alone."*

Queen heaved herself back up to her feet as a circle of cars converged on her. Her body was battered and she ached from head to toe. *I hope no one else on the team finds out I got my ass kicked by a bunch of bumper cars.* As the cars converged, she sprang into the air. The cars came together with a resounding crash, and she came down on top of one. The cars immediately backed up, seeking to keep her hemmed in. She managed to maintain her balance for a moment, and as the car started to whip around, she jumped as high as she could.

The world disappeared and reappeared again and again in

the flickering of the strobe lights, giving her the feeling that she was slowly rising, as if she were floating to the surface of a dark lake. She caught a glimpse of the metal framework above the ride, and grabbed for it. Sharp burrs cut into her hands as she clenched the rusted metal. She swung forward and reached out for another bar, intending to make her way out monkey bar-style.

That was when the strobes went out.

The sudden absence of light blinded Queen, and she found herself holding on with one hand and clutching air with the other. She dangled there until her fumbling hand finally caught hold of another bar and she hung there, listening to the sound of the bumper cars circling in the darkness below. How had a children's ride turned into a school of hungry sharks?

*"I don't understand why you're a concern to Richard Ridley. I assumed you'd be smarter,"* the voice said. *"Don't you know you should never touch the metal over a bumper car ride?"*

The meaning of his words flashed through Queen's mind an instant before a sharp, painful tingling ran down her arms and through her body. She found herself momentarily unable to let go, but the force of her spasms jerked her hands loose, and she hit the ground, her arms and legs twitching and her skin tingling painfully. The voltage had not been sufficient to kill a person, but was just strong enough to drop her to her knees and set her muscles to twitching. Unfortunately for her adversary, it also reminded her of the electric shock torture General Trung inflicted on her before branding her forehead. The memory fueled her anger.

The cars were coming again. She could hear them converging on her from all around. Her night vision returning, she staggered sideways, toward the rail that surrounded the ride, and braced herself for another impact. She was still ten feet from freedom when the ring of cars closed in. She spotted one of the broken-down, overturned cars nearby, and she hurled herself into it, the impact knocking it back down onto its wheels.

Two of the bumper cars smashed into her car, knocking it a few feet toward the side rail. Two more cars struck it, sending her even closer to freedom. She eyed her goal and readied herself to jump for it, but just as she made her move, the car hit a sinkhole in the broken track and upended.

She crashed hard into the rail, but managed to drape one arm over it and haul herself up. More cars were coming, and she rolled over just as they crashed into the fence.

Queen caught her breath for a moment, waiting for the voice to return, but the man stayed silent. "Nothing to say now?" Queen said. She didn't know if the man could hear her, but she said a few choice words about his mother, just in case. Regaining her feet, she was aware of every bump, bruise and scrape on her body. Now she really wanted to hurt someone.

# CHAPTER 10

*They know you're here and they're toying with you. It's not safe. You've confirmed Manifold's presence, and you have sufficient reason to conclude they're conducting experiments on humans. Get out with your ass intact, report to Deep Blue and let him handle it from here. Then you can get back to looking for Rook.* Queen knew she should listen to that small voice in the back of her head, but other parts of her mind were giving counsel as well. *You must be almost there; otherwise, they wouldn't have bothered turning the bumper car ride into a death trap. And why haven't they sent any more men after you? Maybe you're about to breach their last line of defense.* The loudest voice, however, cried out for revenge. That was the one she listened to.

She looked around for another possible way into Manifold's center of operations, and her eyes fell on a revolving swing ride. The platform was elevated several feet off the ground, and up above, the rusted swings hung there, posing no obvious threat. As she moved closer, she saw another trap door, this one larger than the one in the bumper car track, set directly in the ground below the ride deck like a cellar door. It was certainly worth checking.

She took one last look at the ride, trying to spot any sign of danger. Seeing none, she dropped down on all fours and crawled underneath it. Sufficient moonlight glowed through the opening between the central column that supported the ride and the deck that she could see without having to resort to her flashlight. She tried the handle and pulled, but the door did not budge. She gave it another heave, but still no luck. This had to be it! Why else would it be secured? She'd have to blow the door.

Just as she reached that decision, a loud, grinding noise broke the quiet. All around the perimeter of the ride, stainless steel bars six inches apart rose up out of the ground, ringing the deck and imprisoning her in the ride. No matter, she could still climb out through the center, drop a grenade and run. Once the door was blown, she'd climb back in the same way. The thought had just crossed her mind when the center column started to turn. It went slowly at first, picking up speed until it was spinning faster than should have been possible for a swing ride. A sick feeling rose in the pit of her stomach. She supposed she'd better see what was up. She crept over to the column, climbed up the safety wall that ran around the inside of the deck, and peered over the edge.

The swings were bobbing up and down, and from the bottom of each, two razor sharp blades, one on either side, swung back and forth.

*"It's dramatic, I know."* The voice was back. *"But I think you'll find our defenses effective."* All around the deck, spikes intermittently shot up and sank back down. *"You don't need to die here, like this. No soldier of your...skill...deserves a death like this. Give yourself up and live to fight another day."*

Queen scowled. "Go fuck yourself." She'd stick to her plan of blowing the door and seeing what lay behind it.

The man speaking to her sighed and then, as if reading her mind, the door slowly sank out of sight. Queen didn't need to see the oborots to know they were coming—she could hear them. She sprang up onto the edge of the safety rail, balanced there, and looked down at the deck, trying to spot a pattern in the spikes. Seeing a safe spot, she jumped down, drew her pistol, and began picking her way across the deck. She only made it a few steps before the first oborot appeared. The creature perched on the edge of the rail, sniffed the air, and before it could spring, Queen put a bullet in its forehead. The beast fell backward. She hoped it had fallen on the others in its pack, but two more appeared almost instantly. The first one hurled itself at her. Queen got off one shot and deftly sidestepped, dancing around a spike that shot up between her legs. The oborot landed hard on all fours, turned...

...and was impaled by a spike that shot up through its abdomen, splitting its spine. Its cries of pain were ear rending, but Queen didn't have the time or bullets to expend on a mercy killing, because the third oborot was now after her, and she spied a fourth rounding the deck from the opposite side.

Her first shot caught the closest of the beasts in the shoulder, but it didn't slow its charge. Queen sprang onto the body of the fallen oborot, careful to avoid the hole where the spike would soon be reappearing, and jumped again toward the center of the ride. Perhaps she could get back down to the door, though if it led to the oborots' holding pen, she'd be even worse off than she was now.

The oborot tore after her. Another spike shot up, grazing its hairy calf. The thing scarcely noticed the wound, but it slowed down just enough for Queen to take it down with a head shot.

She clambered back over the interior rail, but before she could drop down to the ground, she spotted more oborots coming through the door.

*Road closed. This is getting me a whole lot of nowhere fast.*

She holstered her Mark 23 and jumped up, grabbing hold of a bar on the central column. It was difficult to maintain her grip as the ride spun, but she held on and painstakingly hauled herself up. The oborots quickly came after her. One clawed at her foot and she kicked it away, then stamped down on its head, causing it to lose its grip.

Queen clambered up onto the top of the ride. Bars holding the chairs extended out from the center column like rays of sunlight. Balancing precariously, she clambered out toward the edge of the ride. The farther she moved from the center, the faster the ride spun.

The swings began to bob up and down. Queen held on tight, vowing to find the man who was running this crazy amusement park and castrate him. Behind her, one of the oborots lost its grip and fell to the spiked deck. Queen grimaced at the sight, pleased that one more pursuer was down, but fully aware that a single misstep could doom her to the same fate.

When she could climb no farther, she looked down at the pavement that was flying by at a dizzying rate. Could she make that jump without breaking her neck? The ride continued to spin, and she found herself facing a dense clump of trees. That was it! She waited, ready to launch herself into the trees on the next go-round, hoping the oborots wouldn't get to her before the ride made it back around again. Her perch was so precarious that she didn't dare draw her pistol.

A hairy form moved closer to her, its incredible strength compensating for its lack of climbing ability. Queen's eyes darted from the patch of trees to the oborot and back again to the trees. The deadly ride now felt as if it were turning in slow motion, the trees miles away and the oborot a hair's breadth from dragging her down to her death. The rusted metal cut into her palms as she held on for all she was worth, and the muscles in her back and legs screamed from the pressure of the hunched position she maintained.

The dark outline of the trees came closer.

The oborot reached for her.

And Queen jumped.

Branches tore her skin and clothing as she crashed into the trees. A limb smacked her across the face, and she felt blood pour from her nose. She tumbled down, bouncing like a pinball off every branch, and caught hold of a limb just before she crashed to the ground. The oborots were leaping down off the ride, eager to continue the pursuit. Muttering a curse, Queen dropped to the ground and ran.

The Ferris wheel stood directly in front of her, silently spinning in the darkness. The oborots were almost upon her, so there was no time to wonder what nasty surprise might await her there. She sprang into the closest gondola. Her Mark 23 was in her hand in a flash and she trained it on the closest oborot as it paused, tensing to spring. Two bullets to the head and it was down.

As the gondola rose higher, the oborots were circling the base of the ride, waiting for her to descend. Three of the beasts remained. Queen knew she didn't have the luxury of going round and round, picking them off as she circled. The open gondola would afford her no protection from the beasts. She had to take care of them before she hit the ground.

She considered dropping a grenade on them, but dared not risk it considering the age and condition of the ride. Manifold had obviously made some…improvements to these attractions, but the Ferris wheel supports were clearly old and rusted. She'd have to do this the old-fashioned way.

She leaned out of the gondola, holding on with her left hand and emptied her clip at the first oborot she saw. The beast let out a cry of pain that was so human it gave her a chill, and then it fell in a heap. The gondola descended. Queen slapped in a new clip and chose a new target. The oborot scaled one of the support beams, fully exposing its back to Queen, who took full advantage. Three shots and the beast fell dead to the ground.

*One more to go.*

Queen looked around, but could not see the last remaining oborot. Where had it gone? The Ferris wheel carried her ever closer to the ground as it completed its revolution. Had the oborot fled? Something smashed into the side of the gondola, knocking her sideways. She fell hard into one of the seats and found herself staring into the oborot's grotesque face. The gondola shook from the beast's weight, and Queen's first shot went wide. The second caught it in the shoulder, and it slipped out of sight. The gondola was now on its way up again, and as it rose, she looked out over the edge, seeking to finish off the last remaining beast.

Her eyes pored over the moonlit amusement park for any sign of it, but she saw nothing. Perhaps this one was smarter than the others, and was hiding, waiting to spring when next she made her descent. She watched the world grow smaller as she rose, and as she reached the apex, something grabbed her ankle and yanked her down. She scarcely had time to cry out in surprise before finding herself dangling far above the ground, her weapon gone, clutching the bottom edge of the gondola, inches from the oborot. The thing had caught hold of the gondola as it fell, and now hung by its uninjured left arm, and grabbed for her with its right. Its claw-like fingernails gleamed in the moonlight as it went for her throat.

Queen pulled up and twisted, feeling the beast's nails tear her t-shirt and score her chest. She lashed out with a series of powerful kicks, pummeling the oborot's face and chest. The angry beast swung back, still holding on with one hand. Queen struck the hand with a well-placed kick and the oborot lost its grip. As it fell, it reached out and grabbed hold of her ankle. She felt a jolt as the sudden addition of the beast's weight to her own threatened to rip her shoulders out of their sockets, but Queen was no weakling. They dangled far above the ground, the Ferris wheel slowly descending. Queen looked down and her eyes locked with those of the oborot.

She stamped down with all her might on the oborot's face, and heard the crunch of breaking bone. The beast let out a yelp, lost its grip, and tumbled to the ground. It lay there for a moment, but then managed to rise up on its hands and knees, and started to crawl away.

"Unbelievable," Queen growled. As the gondola came down again, she dropped to the ground and looked around for her lost Mark 23, but she did not see it anywhere. She spotted the oborot. It had regained its feet, and was limping slowly in the direction of the abandoned pirate ride. Queen's eyes flitted to the swing ride, which still spun at a dizzying rate, the swinging blades glinting in the moonlight. The way in was right there, but she'd be cut to pieces before reaching it.

She glanced at the oborot, which seemed to be moving with a purpose. What if it knew another way in? She spared one last moment to look for her Mark 23 and spotted it lying beneath the broken-down wooden steps of the Ferris wheel. She snatched it up and took off in pursuit of the oborot.

It hobbled past the remains of the boat swing ride and vanished into a thick stand of weeds and shrubbery on the other side. Queen got there just in time to see it disappear into an old storm drain. Taking a deep breath, she followed, hoping it would not lead her to a dead end...or into a death trap.

# CHAPTER 11

"Where the hell did she go?" Darius watched as Andrew clicked on the various cameras, trying to locate the woman. Damn Manifold and the shoestring budget they'd put him on. One little mistake and he was in the doghouse. Hell, he was in the outhouse. He needed this project to succeed to get back into Ridley's good graces, not that he'd heard from the man in months.

"She ran past the ship swing ride," Andrew said. His tone said, not for the first time, that he disapproved of the money Darius had spent modifying the old amusement park. "If she doesn't change direction, we should see her on camera five shortly."

"That's a big 'if.' She's surprised me so far. No reason to expect she won't do it again." Darius hated admitting that, but the woman had proved to be resourceful and downright ferocious. He wouldn't have believed it from looking at her. With that face and body, she belonged in a magazine, not the military.

"Maybe she's bugging out," Andrew said hopefully.

"It's possible." Darius stroked his chin, feeling the rough stubble. "I would prefer she not escape, though."

"I could release the remainder of the failed test groups. That one small pack almost finished her." There was a manic glow in Andrew's eyes. "They're bouncing off the walls as it is. We've already determined their minds can't be restored. If we're going to kill them anyway…"

"No." Darius slashed the air with his hand, cutting off Andrew's words. "Think. What would happen if they got to civilization before daybreak?"

Andrew shrugged. "Some civilians would be killed, but by the time the police track down the culprits, regression will have kicked in and they'll arrest some raving lunatics, that's all."

"A bunch of lunatics all just happen to terrorize the same part of the country on the same night? And what if there are witnesses? One person telling the story would be dismissed. But several people all telling the same tale is a different story. We'd be shut down for certain, and if the law didn't get us, Ridley would."

"Accidents happen, things don't work out. Ridley should understand that." If Andrew had ever met Richard Ridley, the head of Manifold Genetics, he would not dismiss the thought so casually.

"We're *not* letting them out, and that's final. Just keep an eye out for her and let me know when she shows her face. I'll track her down myself."


**The storm** drain was a tight squeeze, and Queen muttered a prayer of thanks that she wasn't some bulky heifer. She followed the sound of the oborot, her pistol held out in front of her should she need it. A fetid odor hung in the air, blending with the dank, moldy smell of the old drain. Her hand came down on something cold and gooey. She yanked her hand back and wiped it on the side of the drain, getting rid of the worst of the ooze. Taking out her flashlight and cupping her hand around it to minimize the light, she shined it on the floor. A rotting arm laid there, the flesh almost completely liquefied.

*Nice*, she thought. *At least I know why it stinks in here.* She wondered if more stray body parts waited up ahead.

She crawled another twenty feet until she finally put her hand down onto...nothing. A portion of the floor a good two feet across had fallen away. Her light revealed that the fissure dropped down a few feet to an air duct that had been torn open. She wondered if the first oborot she had encountered had escaped this way, or if it had been released for a purpose.

She didn't love the idea of climbing into an air duct, but if an oborot could pass through without getting stuck or bringing the vent crashing down, so could she. It was crucial, however, that she did not wind up in the middle of their holding pen or whatever place it was they called home. Holding her finger on the trigger of her Mark 23, she slithered head first down into the vent. Up ahead, the way was lit by the glow of light shining through vents in the bottom of the duct. Careful to make no noise, she crept up to the first vent and peered through.

A slender man in a lab coat leaned in close to a computer monitor, blocking her view of the screen. He was muttering something. She strained to hear what he was saying, and made out the words, "Where is she?"

"You still haven't located her?" A deep voice called from somewhere out of sight. She gritted her teeth, recognizing the voice of the man who had taunted her while trying to kill her with his sicko rides.

"No, but there are plenty of places she could hide. I'll keep watching."

"Let me know when she resurfaces. I want to take her out before she makes it out of the city."

The man at the computer turned around to face the speaker, giving her a clear view of his face. He was young, perhaps in his late twenties, clean-cut—the stereotypical laboratory squint. Only his eyes, sparkling with a dark, twisted zeal, marred his otherwise benign appearance. "She's already taken out our entire security detail. Watch yourself."

Queen grinned. *That was a helpful bit of information.*

"She won't find *me* so easy to deal with." The voice was so smug and self-assured that Queen had to fight the sudden urge to kick the vent loose, drop down into the middle of the room, and take him on right then and there. *Play it smart. They don't know you're here, so use that to your advantage.*

She heard footsteps as the second man walked away, and the young squint turned back to his computer. Satisfied she wouldn't hear anything else of value here, at least not right away, she moved farther down the shaft.

The next vent overlooked a hallway. She couldn't see far enough in either direction to discern if it would be a safe place to exit, so she kept moving. Finally she came to a vent above a small storage room. The walls were lined with shelves packed with a variety of chemicals and laboratory supplies. She quickly took hold of the vent cover with both hands and tested it. It was held in place by clips that slid free with the scantest scrape of metal on metal, though in the silence it sounded to Queen like a car crash. Setting the vent aside, she dropped nimbly into the room...

...just as the door opened.

A balding man with graying temples walked in. He was staring down at a clipboard and did not see her until she thrust her gun in his face and pressed her free hand over his mouth. He gave a muffled whimper and let the clipboard clatter to the floor. Behind his thick glasses, his eyes, wide with fright, gave him the look of a startled owl.

"Do you speak English?" she whispered. The man nodded. "If you answer my questions and don't try to call for help, I'll let you live. You do anything at all I don't like, you die slowly and painfully. Got it?"

The man nodded and Queen uncovered his mouth, but kept the gun trained on him.

"Is this place safe for us to talk?" she whispered.

"Perhaps," he replied in a soft voice. "Our directors are in their offices and seldom have reason to come this way. And security…" He shrugged. "I have not seen them in the last hour or so. They all seem to be outside."

"Don't worry about security. Tell me, is this place run by Manifold Genetics?"

The man blanched at the name. "Yes, but how did you know?"

"That doesn't matter. Fill me in on what's going on here." Her trigger finger itched. She wanted to get busy cleaning house, but it was important to learn as much as she could about what Manifold was up to and what, exactly, they'd managed to accomplish. "Are you making these oborots, or werewolves, or whatever they are?"

The man swallowed hard. "We should go to my office. If someone should pass by this place and hear my voice, they might investigate and there is nowhere for you to hide. They are accustomed to hearing me talk to myself or to the subjects when I am working in my office. It will be safer there."

"Is it far?" Queen wondered if he was up to something, but she saw no deceit in his eyes. In any case, she couldn't stay here forever. Sooner or later, she'd have to risk it.

"Not far. You can put on one of the lab coats." He indicated a stack of neatly folded white coats. "It will be less noticeable than what you have on. My colleague is about your size and her hair is only a little darker. As long as no one gets a good look at you, they will probably take you for her at a glance."

"She's not going to come walking in on us, is she?"

The man's face darkened and he shook his head. "She will not interrupt us, no." There was something he wasn't telling her. He looked up at her and frowned. Queen thought he had noticed the skull brand on her forehead, but then he explained. "You should probably wash the dirt off of your face."

Keeping her weapon trained on the man, Queen grabbed a

container of germicidal wipes and gave herself a quick scrub. This time he did notice the brand, and his eyes widened, but he made no comment.

"You have a name?" Queen asked as she removed her small pack, stuffed it into a medical waste bag, slipped into the lab coat, and buttoned it over her ragged t-shirt.

"Slifko." His voice was tight and scratchy.

"All right, Slifko, let's get this straight. You are to lead me straight to your office. If you try anything at all, you're a dead man. My gun is up my sleeve and aimed at the center of your back, but know this," she stepped in close and the taller man seemed to shrink before her, "I don't need a gun to take care of you."

Slifko nodded, sweat beading on his forehead and his complexion going from fair to pallid. "I understand," he gasped.

It was a short walk down a quiet hallway of unrelenting white to Slifko's office. They did not encounter a soul, and when Queen closed the door behind her, she allowed herself to relax just a little. Above the fastidiously organized desk on the far side of the room, a row of monitors hung on the wall, each displaying a roomful of holding cells, Each cell housed an oborot. Queen did not have time to examine them closely, but she could see at a glance the obvious differences between the various groups. Some were fully bestial, fine hair and rippled muscles coating their bodies. These were enraged, pounding or hurling themselves at the walls of their cells. Others retained more of their human traits, with only a moderate amount of body hair.

"Time to sing, little bird." Queen motioned at Slifko with the barrel of her gun. When her order was met with a puzzled expression, she dropped the idiom. "Tell me about this place. Why is it here and what are you trying to do?"

Slifko cleared his throat and began his explanation.

"I worked at Pripyat Hospital when the disaster at Chernobyl occurred. I was at work when soldiers came for me. They told me of the accident and said I was needed to tend to one of the victims. I presumed the person was merely an injured worker and was puzzled that they had not brought him directly to the hospital. What I found was something very different." His eyes took on a faraway cast and, Queen thought, a gleam of excitement. "A worker at the Chernobyl plant had been exposed to a heavy dose of radiation and was undergoing what could only be described as a transformation. He looked like the subjects you see here." He pointed to the monitor that showed the most violent group. "It was the most fascinating discovery of my career—a condition like none I had ever seen." She could hear the wonder in his voice and it turned her stomach.

"Why you?" Queen could not keep the distaste from her voice. The man clearly had no regard whatsoever for his human subjects. "Was it the luck of the draw, or was there a particular reason they chose you?"

"My reputation preceded me. I have always been drawn to the legend of the oborot. Years ago, I came across a journal, written in the thirteenth century, by a man named Kurek. He recounted the story of his friend being killed by an oborot-like creature. It happened in this region. Furthermore, he told of dark rumors regarding the families in this area. I believe most legends have a basis in scientific fact, and I was convinced there was something to Kurek's account. I focused my research on the area around Pripyat and Chernobyl. In time, I came to be known by some as the crazy wolf hunter." He stared at the monitors, lost in memory. "We took him to a secure facility and observed him. I did not have sufficient resources to determine what caused his condition, but I was now certain that the oborot could exist. Rather, that a condition existed that explained the legend. Perhaps the traits had been lying dormant in his genes until exposure to just the right amount of radiation brought about the change." He continued to gaze at the screens. "So I learned all I could about the man and his ancestors. They were from this area, and were one of those families that had been regarded with suspicion, if not outright fear. I was on to something, but I could do little more though, without adequate facilities and funding. I needed financial support for my research."

"I can think of a few snags you might have hit," Queen said.

"More than a few." Slifko nodded. "Under the old Soviet government, I tried approaching various elements through intermediaries, but without success. After the fall, I made similar inquiries to corporations, but was met with outright scorn. It was a long time before I found a man who took my work seriously."

"Richard Ridley." The name was bitter on Queen's lips. The sick bastard already had much to answer for, and here was yet another example of his evil at work.

"Correct. I do not think he held out great hope for my work but I had enough research to convince him it was a worthwhile investment. He granted me a modest budget and set us up in the shadow of Chernobyl in a place close enough to find subjects for study, but also a place where we were unlikely to be discovered."

"Hiding in plain sight." Queen frowned. Something he had said bothered Queen. "What do you mean by 'close enough to find subjects to study'?" The malice in her voice was unmistakable, and Slifko took a step back.

"Subject Alpha, that's what I labeled the first patient, hails from this region. I was able to study other members of his family, and that is how I made my breakthrough. Once I learned what was going on inside their bodies, I was able to initiate those changes in test subjects."

"What happens to them? Obviously they don't turn into wolves."

"No, nothing so mysterious." Slifko settled down on the counter that ran the length of the left-hand wall. If he still felt himself in danger, his enthusiasm for his subject seemed to have overcome it. "You have, of course, heard the many stories of people who, under extreme duress, do amazing things? Lift a car off a loved one, for example." Queen nodded and indicated he should continue. "This is caused by contraction of the deep fascia, a thin, fibrous membrane that holds our musculature in place. Our fight or flight response, for example, involves a temporary increase in the stiffness of the deep fascia, which allows us to perform those feats of strength and speed that greatly surpass our normal capabilities."

"I know all about this," Queen growled, reaching into the medical waste bag and removing a thumb drive from her backpack. "Move on. I don't have much time, and you're beginning to bore me." She gave him a cool look. "You'll find I'm not the most patient audience, and you won't like my heckling one bit."

Slifko's eyes darted to the barrel of the Mark 23, now aimed at his groin, and gasped. "Yes, of course." He took a moment to compose himself. "How and why the deep fascia contracts is not completely understood, but in the case of our subjects, it involves agitation of the myofibroblasts."

"Which are?" Queen moved to the computer and settled into the swivel chair, still keeping an eye on Slifko.

"A myofibroblast is a cell that carries some of the proper-ties of a smooth muscle cell, the ability to contract, for example, and the properties of a fibroblast, a cell that serves many functions. Fibroblasts provide structure for connective tissue, produce and secrete fibers and play a critical role in cell main-tenance and metabolism, particularly in healing."

Queen inserted the thumb drive into the computer, switched her weapon to her left hand so she could use the mouse with her right, and double-clicked on the icon that popped up. The program was a simple one that would search out and copy all data files from the computer, and any part of the server, to the thumb drive while also initiating an upload of the same data through a satellite uplink. It wouldn't bypass the better firewalls, but it was a useful tool when time was at a premium.

"What are you doing?" Slifko scowled.

"Don't worry about me, just keep talking." The program now initiated, Queen turned back to Slifko. "You know, myofibroblasts, werewolves, sicko experiments on human subjects. Make me understand. Your life depends on it."

Slifko's Adam's apple looked like a buoy bobbing in rough water as he attempted to swallow his fear. "Under certain circumstances, the number of myofibroblasts inside our subjects' bodies multiplied substantially, and entered an agitated state of contraction, resulting in an extreme and prolonged contraction of the deep fascia, granting them strength and speed bordering on the superhuman." His eyes darted to the computer screen where the upload had begun, and then back to Queen. "Unlike those brief feats of heroic strength that people perform in emergency situations, this state can last for hours at a time."

"Is it caused by the full moon?" Queen smirked.

"Yes, at least that is the most common inducement, and it is one of the things we do not fully understand. For some time now, the medical community has used photobiomodulation, or low-level laser therapy, to stimulate healing. We know that through specific wavelengths, fibroblasts can be transformed into myofibroblasts. In our subjects, something in the moon-light actually causes the fibroblasts to *produce* myofibroblasts and send them into a state of contraction."

"Wait a minute." Queen held up her hand. "Moonlight is just reflected sunlight. If it's nothing more than a certain wavelength of light causing this, it should happen in sunlight as well."

"The moon is not a perfect mirror. It reflects unevenly, due to absorption of certain wavelengths. We believe that something in the full spectrum of sunlight serves to balance out the wavelengths that initiate the creation of the myofibroblasts, and suppresses the reaction."

"What about the hair growth? Some of these people really look like werewolves." Queen inclined her head toward the monitors.

"The reaction stimulates the rapid growth of vellus hair, the fine hair that grows all over our bodies beginning in childhood. We assume it is a side effect of the fibroblasts' metabolic functions. With our limited budget, we have focused on the strength and speed effects. Excess body hair is not a hindrance, so we have not studied it."

"Are all these people related to Subject Alpha?" Queen reminded herself that these were not merely beasts, but human victims of Manifold Genetics.

"Oh no. We have very few of those subjects. These are people in whom we have been able to replicate the condition, and even stimulate it through the use of artificial light." He saw the fire in Queen's eyes and hurried on, hands raised in a defensive posture. "Please understand, we are not kidnappers pulling people off the streets to perform experiments on them. The first subjects, those from Subject Alpha's genetic pool, were volunteers who hoped we could find a cure. They were well-paid. Since then, all our subjects have been prisoners: murderers, rapists, the lowest of the low. Darius, our director, secured them for us."

"Did you snatch a boy from the streets tonight? A dark-haired kid about eighteen?"

"I don't think so. Understand, I do not secure the subjects. Darius sees to that."

Queen didn't like it. Even if the guy was telling the truth, who was he to turn human beings into raving beasts?

"I'm assuming Manifold isn't interested in turning people into werewolves. You must have promised them you could produce super-strong, super-fast soldiers."

"We are almost there," Slifko said. "The subjects, however, lose their minds during the transformation, and become crazed, much like the oborots, or werewolves, of legend. After regression, some of the madness remains. The more frequently they transform, the more they lose of themselves when they are in their normal state. After enough transformations, the person is reduced to an animal-like state. When we can eliminate those problems, we will have succeeded." He shook his head. "If Darius did not waste precious funding on his so-called defense systems, our progress would be much more rapid."

"Those defense systems wouldn't involve turning carnival rides into killing machines, would they?"

Slifko nodded. "Darius is not a scientist. I am told he is former military, and his assignment here is a punishment for something he did that upset Richard Ridley. I do not know much about the man, but I know he is not quite right in the head. I sometimes think he wants us to succeed so that he himself can enjoy the benefits. He often wonders aloud what a group of elite soldiers with the oborot's strength and speed could do."

Queen thought of the experiments Manifold had performed using the DNA of the hydra in hopes of producing soldiers whose bodies could heal any wound. Just like this situation, Manifold had not found a way to control the accompanying madness. She imagined what would happen if the flaws in both experiments were corrected. Regenerating soldiers were bad enough, but regenerating soldiers with superhuman strength and speed? It was unthinkable.

"Have there been many escapes?"

"Occasionally, but we have always managed to kill or recapture them. We do not know how the escapes happen, though."

"Air vent," Queen said. "I followed one back inside."

Slifko frowned. "That is impossible! We would have noticed the missing vent cover!"

"Do your cameras point at the ceiling?"

"No." Slifko shook his head. "But when we feed them or come in to conduct research, surely we would notice a vent cover lying on the ground."

"Maybe they remove the cover at the beginning of the transformation, when they're mostly human, and replace it after regression. You can't watch every cell closely all night long."

"Why not escape, then? That would be crazy."

"They *are* crazy, Doctor. Your experiments drove them insane."

Slifko hung his head. "You sound like my colleague, Doctor Danilchuk. She no longer supported what we do here."

"What happened to her?"

"Darius would not let her leave. When she vowed to go in spite of him, he…" Slifko's eyes drifted to the monitors on the wall.

"He turned her into a test subject? Unbelievable." Shaking her head, Queen looked away from Slifko and noticed that the upload was finished. She reached down to retrieve her thumb drive.

It was Slifko's reflection in the computer screen that did him in.

Queen saw a flash of movement as the scientist came at her, his arm upraised. She whirled about and caught his wrist, the needle of a syringe inches from her face. Slifko scarcely had time to cry out before she pressed her gun to the soft flesh below his chin and fired. The silenced round sounded like an explosion in the quiet room, but it was nothing compared to what she was about to do. It was time to burn this place to the ground.

# CHAPTER 12

Andrew cried out in surprise and fell out of his chair when the first explosion tore apart the far end of the corridor. Coated in dust, ears ringing, he staggered to his feet and leaned heavily against his desk. His first thought was there had been an accident, but that couldn't be. The explosion came from the direction of Slifko's office. He didn't conduct experiments in there, and anyway, what did he even have in the labs that could explode?

Then he remembered the woman. She was coming. It had to be her.

He rummaged through the desk drawer and found the 9mm pistol he'd been issued on his first day on the job. His hands were trembling so violently that it took him two tries to get the pistol out of the holster. He checked to make sure it was still loaded. He'd had plenty of training with the weapon, but that had been at the beginning of his employment with Manifold. Now he felt like he'd never seen a gun before.

Another explosion, this one closer, rocked his office and he dropped the gun. It clattered across the tile floor and slid out of sight beneath a rolling cart. He hurried over and retrieved it, all the while saying a prayer of thanks that it had not gone off. The safety must have been on, or did that even matter?

The safety! What was it? What did it look like? In his panic, he found he could remember nothing about the weapon. Hell, he might as well ditch the gun and find somewhere to hide until Darius showed up. If he showed up. *Quit being such an idiot*, he told himself. *You can do this!* He found a button on the side and slid it to what appeared to be the firing position. Already he was feeling more confident. Now, should he hold it in two hands like on the cop shows, or hold it sideways in one hand, gang-banger style? He decided on the two-handed grip. It felt steadier. Holding the pistol out in front of him, he stepped around the corner.

A dark figure moved wraithlike through the dust and debris that hung in the air. Instinctively, Andrew pulled the trigger. The gun jerked wildly in his hands, and his shot blew out a light in the ceiling halfway down the hall. The figure moved closer and he recognized the woman they had seen on the security video. She didn't bat an eye, but slowly leveled her own pistol at him. He cried out, half in challenge, half in fear, and pulled the trigger repeatedly, firing off a rapid barrage. When the last round was expended, he kept pulling the trigger, as if he could squeeze one more round from the empty clip.

And then he heard a loud pop, and thought for a moment that he had, indeed, gotten off another shot, but he was already flying backward. He hit the ground and pain like he never dreamed possible burned through every inch of his body, radiating out from his gut. He screamed until he thought his vocal cords would tear in two.

He sensed, rather than heard, the woman's approach. He looked up to see her looming over him, her pistol in one hand and a knife in the other, its razor edge gleaming in the artificial light. She was beautiful, with golden hair and eyes of deep indigo. And then he saw the angry skull branded in her forehead. His lips moved, but he could not cry out. With a supreme effort of will, he raised his empty pistol, but she kicked it out of his hand.

"You're not Darius, are you?" She spoke through gritted teeth that, in his pain and stupor, looked to Andrew like fangs.

He shook his head. "No, I'm Andrew. I just do computers and stuff like that."

"But you work here, don't you?"

He sensed he should lie, make up some sort of story that would paint him as an innocent victim, but he found he could not. Her eyes held him mesmerized and her terrible beauty compelled him to tell the truth. "Yes, I do."

"So you are partly responsible for these experiments on humans. You helped turn them into monsters."

He nodded. The woman, her expression unchanging, kicked him. Fire erupted between his legs but the pain of the gunshot rendered it negligible. He tried to draw his knees up to his chest but he lacked the strength.

"That's a nasty wound," she said, motioning to the bullet hole in his stomach. "It will take about fifteen minutes, but it's going to kill you. You don't deserve the time, but if you believe in God, now's your chance to make your peace." The last thing he saw of her was her blonde hair swinging to and fro.

Despair turned to bitterness as the inevitability of his death took hold in his mind. This couldn't be happening! Their security force, Darius's tricks and Darius himself, should have been enough to stop a solitary woman. What had happened to Darius, anyway? Why hadn't he come to Andrew's aid? Darius had left him to fend for himself, probably hiding or even running away to save his own neck. Well, they could all kiss his ass. Andrew wouldn't be the only one to die this day.

With strength borne of bitterness and despair, he rolled over onto his stomach and crawled to his desk, leaving a thick smear of blood on the white tile. Pain and loss of blood made him dizzy, but he managed to haul himself up far enough that he was able to reach his computer mouse and keyboard. A few clicks, a single command, and it was done.

She'd be begging God for mercy long before he did.

Andrew grinned at the thought of every remaining oborot running loose on a turning night, with hours left until dawn.

Something clattered behind him and he looked back to see a dark object the size of a baseball bouncing toward him. Then the world erupted in a blinding flash and he was dead, torn apart by a grenade before his body could send pain signals to his mind.

**Movement out** of the corner of her eye caused Queen to hit the ground and roll. The air above her was alive with a sound like hypersonic hornets, and the wall behind her was torn apart. A Metal Storm weapon! She'd had enough of these things to last a lifetime. She looked for a target but the shooter had already ducked around the far corner out of sight. She did the same, sliding back into the hallway.

"You should have taken my offer." The voice was the same one that had taunted her in the amusement park.

"You must be Darius," she replied

"My reputation precedes me. I'm flattered."

Her mind raced for a solution. She was outgunned and had no cover to mask her approach. She could pitch a grenade down the hall, but he was likely to be expecting that, and would clear out long before it went off. She could follow the hall and see what lay in the direction away from the computer lab she had just blown up. She could continue her destruction and force him to pursue her. Of course, he knew this place better than she did, and she might just walk into yet another trap. She gritted her teeth. Caution of any kind was not her usual M.O., but she was determined to stay alive for two reasons: to get revenge for Armina and to find out what happened to Rook.

"So, what brings you here? How did you find us?"

Queen thought the question was odd. He had to know that Manifold Gamma, Beta and Alpha had been compromised and that Richard Ridley no longer ran the company. But if he didn't, that information might be more powerful than any bullet. "You haven't heard, have you?" she called down the hall.

The man didn't reply. He was no doubt trying to figure out her angle.

"Manifold has been shut down," she said. "Richard Ridley is dead."

"Bullshit," the man said quickly.

"When was the last time you heard from him?"

No reply.

"We found your location thanks to intel recovered from one of the Manifold facilities."

"Ridley would have destroyed the—"

"Ridley fell out of a helicopter. Two hundred feet. Hit every branch on the way down. He was in pieces when we found his body." This was only partly true. Ridley had actually jumped out of the helicopter and all they'd recovered was his arm. He reappeared again, more dangerous than before, but they'd taken him out for good—buried him under a mountain. But Darius didn't need to know all that. All that mattered was that Ridley wouldn't be coming back. "Think about it. How else could we have found you?"

No retort answered her question. Darius might or might not believe her, but he wasn't giving up the fight. Quick as a flash, he swung around the corner, aiming his Metal Storm weapon in her direction. Queen had been waiting for the attack though, and she managed to fire off a single round and duck back before another hail of projectiles shredded the wall a few feet above where she had lain. She'd had only the briefest glance at her enemy, but now she had a visual to go with the voice: a tall, barrel of a man with pale skin, a long toucan beak of a nose, and scars crisscrossing his shaved head.

"Not a bad shot for a girl." She took satisfaction at the note of pain underlying his forced bravado. "You winged me, but it's just a scratch. Want to try again? You should be able to hit a big target like me."

She remained silent. He would be wondering if he'd gotten her. Perhaps, if she played dead, she could induce him to come her way. Get him halfway down the hall with nowhere to hide and he was hers.

"Why so quiet? Did I hurt your feelings? Come now, I gave you free rides on my amusements, the least you can do is talk to me." His laugh was deep and rich; it was a sound that, in another time and place and coming from another person, might have raised her spirits. Now, it only served to fuel her ire. "You're playing possum, now, aren't you?" he called. "I thought you were braver than that."

Still she kept her silence. She was about to go with plan B, and sneak back down the hall behind her, blowing shit up, when Darius cried out in surprise and another burst of fire echoed through the hallway. Wary of a trap, Queen crawled back to the corner, but then she heard an inhuman snarling sound, and she knew what was happening before she even saw it.

Darius was rolling on the ground, locked in combat with an oborot almost as big as him. This was her chance. She charged full-bore at the two combatants, firing at them as she ran. The way she saw it, it did not matter which of them she hit. Darius had to die for what he and the others had done here. The oborots, even after they returned to their fully human states, were doomed to lives of madness, interspersed with monthly transformations into mindless, violent monsters. Killing them would be a mercy.

She was halfway down the hall when something crashed into her from behind. She went down under a heavy weight, and just managed to twist around so that she landed on her side instead of flat on her face. The sound of Darius's fight with the oborot had masked the approach of another of the creatures, and it had chased her down from behind. Her gun hand was pinned beneath her body but her knife hand was free. She drove an elbow into its jaw and followed with a slash to the throat. It was a shallow cut, but the oborot drew back, roaring in surprise and pain. Now that she understood what the creature was, she could see the human being behind the monster. Its eyes, however, were pure beast, and it would not stop until it killed her. The creature swiped at her, its fingers held like claws, and its nails raked across her cheek. Queen slashed again, opening a gash across the oborot's thickly muscled abdomen. The oborot rocked back and raised its head as it roared in pain. She reversed the knife and plunged it into the beast's heart. The oborot rolled off her and her knife was yanked from her grip as the creature struggled to pull the blade free. Queen sat up, leveled her Mark 23, and took out the Oborot with a single shot to the temple.

Before she could move, a shadow loomed over her and someone gave her gun hand a vicious kick, knocking her weapon from her grasp. She rolled underneath another kick and came to her feet facing Darius.

His eyes, alive with malice, seemed to glow against his skin. The scars on his head lent to his sinister air. He stood tensed, ready to attack, his hands opening and closing as if eager to crush her.

"Thanks for getting that thing off of me. If you'd been a better shot you might have killed it." He circled to Queen's left. Her gun was somewhere behind her, and doubtless he would love to get his hands on it. "The damn thing took off with my gun if you can believe it. A few of them are cleverer than the others. It didn't know what the hell the gun was, I'm sure, but it carried it away all the same. I hope it wraps its mouth around the barrel." He smiled as Queen moved in lock step with him, keeping herself between him and the gun she didn't dare turn around to look for. "That just means I get to kill you with my bare hands. I'm going to like that." His pearly white teeth glistened as he smiled.

The man outweighed her by more than a hundred pounds,

but Queen was not the least bit intimidated. She wasn't the first woman in special ops for nothing, and she relished hand-to-hand combat. She especially loved the look in the eyes of a bigger opponent the moment he realized he was being beaten by a cute little girl. In fact, she'd made quite an impression on Chess Team leader Jack Sigler, call sign: King, when she sparred with him for ten brutal rounds. Afterward, he had invited her to join his squad.

"A little less conversation, a little more action," she said. With that, Queen sprang into motion, striking out with a quick jab that snapped his head back. Darius recovered instantly, and caught her wrist as she followed with a right cross. She yanked back, freeing herself from his powerful grip and ducked too late to evade his hook. The blow glanced off the top of her head and made her ears ring, but she'd been hit harder in her lifetime. Much harder.

Darius waded in, throwing punches with sufficient force to cave in Queen's skull should any of them find their mark. She evaded them and struck back with a leg kick to the inside of his front knee. A low grunt was the only indicator that he'd felt any kind of pain. For her part, Queen hoped she hadn't fractured a bone in her foot. The man's legs were like tree trunks.

She slipped another of his punches, flattened her hand like the blade of a knife, and drove her fingertips into his eye. Darius roared and swung a wild back fist that she took in the shoulder, but it was still powerful enough to stagger her. Sensing an advantage, Darius charged.

Queen spun out of the way and tripped Darius as he passed, sending him tumbling to the ground. She realized a split-second too late that this was what he had been counting on. He hadn't been trying to take her down at all. He was going for her gun!

She leaped onto his back just as he was rising up on all fours. Lightning fast, she locked her legs about his waist, clamped her arm around his neck, and squeezed. She felt him try to tuck his chin but he was too late. Her arm was over his windpipe, and she was putting all she had into the choke.

She expected him to roll over and try to fight his way out of the chokehold, but instead he slowly, but surely, climbed to his feet. He was stronger than she would have believed. He took hold of her arm with both hands and pulled. Queen held on with everything she had, knowing it was now a race against time. If Darius managed to break her grip before he lost consciousness, she might be too spent to keep up the fight.

Darius thrashed about, making Queen feel like she was riding a bucking bronco. Then, without warning, he hurled himself backward, slamming Queen into the wall. Her backpack lessened the impact slightly, but the air was forced from her lungs in a rush. *I can't catch a break,* she thought as she gasped for breath. Darius dashed her against the wall again and her head struck, sending a torrent of pain shooting through her skull and down her spine.

*He's got to be almost out by now,* she thought, and tightened her grip on his thickly muscled neck. Her arms burned from exertion and her head felt like Humpty Dumpty after the great fall.

Darius staggered forward and let go of her arm with his right hand, still working with his left to loosen her grip. For a moment, Queen thought he was losing consciousness, but then her eyes fell on what lay on the floor a few steps away. Her Mark 23. If Darius got hold of it, he'd kill her, and if she released her grip on him, there was no way she'd beat him to the weapon.

"Oh hell no you don't!" Nearly out of options, she bit down on his ear as hard as she could. Salty blood filled her mouth as her teeth bit through flesh and sank into gristle. Darius grabbed at her head, all thoughts of the gun forgotten. She shook her head back and forth like a pit bull. Darius's fingers brushed her head, but his strength was ebbing fast. He made a low, wheezing sound and, at long last, sank to the ground unconscious.

Queen rolled off the man, spat out a mouthful of blood and gristle, and lay gasping on the floor. Every muscle in her body felt like water. She was spent, but she had to go on. Still panting from exertion, she stood on trembling legs and recovered her weapon. She spotted the handle of her knife jutting from the chest of the oborot and she moved to retrieve it when she heard the most unwelcome sound imaginable.

Oborots were coming.

Lots of them.

# CHAPTER 13

Spewing every curse she could think of, Queen took off running away from the sound of the pursuing beasts. She turned a corner, burst through the double-doors that barred her way, and found herself in a laboratory. Every metal surface was polished to a high sheen, and walls, ceiling and floor were all snow white. To think such evil could have been done here was beyond her ability to comprehend.

Lining the shelves to her left were glass containers where brains and other body parts were preserved. Beside the shelf were industrial sized containers of formaldehyde. She knew what she had to do.

Her eyes alit on an emergency exit on the opposite side of the room, and she breathed a sigh of relief. She made a beeline for it, reaching into her pack as she ran and fishing out another grenade. She broke through the door and found herself in a deep, narrow concrete shaft. A single security light glowed a sickly yellow, revealing iron rungs leading up to the trapdoor. Queen made some hasty calculations and, without allowing time for second thoughts, activated the grenade, pitched it back into the lab in the midst of the containers of formaldehyde, and started to climb.

One...

Her palms seemed to stick to the cold metal as she climbed.

Two...

Her arms, weakened by the fight with Darius, moved robotically, driven more by her determination than by any remaining strength.

Three...

She had perhaps two seconds remaining before the grenade blew, and she was only halfway to the top. Roaring out a battle cry, she clambered up like a spider, recklessly hurling herself from rung-to-rung. If she lost her grip, she would die.

Four...

Her eyes locked on the trapdoor looming tantalizingly just out of reach. She thought of Rook, and wondered if he was alive and, if so, would he try to find out what happened to her. She reached for the latch to unlock the trapdoor.

Five...

She released the latch and pushed the door open just as the explosion ripped through the lab. The force hurled her out into the cool night air, and she fell hard to the ground.

Queen stood and looked at the smoke that poured from the open trapdoor. She took no comfort in the sight. Armina was still dead, and those wretched souls upon whom Darius and Slifko had performed their sick experiments were doomed to lives as insane killing machines. She wondered if Deep Blue would find a way to notify the authorities of what lived in the underground lab or if he would take other measures. The oborots had to be put down for their own sakes and for those of the innocent people they might victimize.

She took a few deep breaths and tried to collect herself. After a minute's rest, she was ready to move on. That was when the first beastly head poked up out of the escape shaft.

The oborots had braved the burning lab and, once again, they were coming for her.

She turned and ran, dashing with reckless abandon through the darkened streets, her mind racing faster than her feet. The shortest path of escape would be east, directly to the port where she had arranged for a boat to meet her. She glanced back and saw more oborots joining the chase. She wondered if all the remaining beasts were on her trail. Probably. They had to smell the blood, her own and that of others, on her. She resigned herself to the fact that she now had to outwit an entire pack of crazed creatures that wanted her blood.

The boat that awaited her would be patrolling the port, the pilot keeping an eye out for her. Unless he was waiting near the shore at exactly the place where she made her appearance though, there was no way she could hold off an entire pack while waiting for the boat to reach her. *Time for plan B.*

She veered to her right, sprinting through the town square. It was oddly named, she thought, because it was shaped more like half an oval, with one end enclosed by a circular wall with a drive cutting through the center. Here, throngs of people had once dined at the Polesie Restaurant, stayed in its companion hotel and milled through the Pripyat shopping center. Despite her dire circumstances, it still struck her as odd to consider that this ghost town had once teemed with life.

Up ahead, three oborots rounded the corner of the shopping center and came for her. Wondering how they had managed to get in front of her, Queen turned and dashed into Energetik, Pripyat's so-called palace of culture. This place had once been the city's center of community life, featuring concert and dance halls, a library, a gymnasium and a swimming pool. She sprinted through the bare hallways, the glow of the full moon through broken windows and holes in the walls providing scant light by which she navigated around and over the scattered books, tiles and debris that choked the floor. She stole a glance back to see the three creatures closing in on her, but the rest of the pack was not in sight. At least, not yet.

She turned a corner and dashed down the wide hallway.

The oborots were closing fast. Soon she would be forced to make a fight of it. She could shed her backpack to gain a little more speed, but she needed what it held—and not just the remaining grenades—to make her getaway.

Up ahead, broken doors, hanging askew from twisted hinges welcomed her into a room lined all around with dingy, broken white tiles. The swimming pool lay directly in front of her, the shallow end giving way to a deep diving area on the far end. She circled the pool and sprinted alongside it, the oborots so close she could hear their every breath and the distinctive sound of their hairy footfalls on the hard tile floor.

She reached the far end of the pool, cut a sharp left, took two steps, and leaped. Her stomach turned somersaults as the floor fell out from underneath her. She reached out and grabbed the edge of the diving board. As her momentum swung her forward, the oborots flew past her, falling in a pile to the bottom of the empty diving pool. Queen hauled herself up onto the diving board, drew her pistol, and put a bullet into the skull of each of the writhing beasts.

Her shoulders sagged and she exhaled a long, ragged sigh, but her relief was short-lived. She heard the distant sounds of the pack of oborots and knew that somewhere in the depths of the palace of culture, the others were back on her trail.

She vaulted a rail on the far side of the room and exited through a gaping hole that had once been a plate glass window. She hit the ground in the midst of tangled undergrowth, broken glass and shattered tile. Looming above her, she could see the silhouette of her destination.

Nicknamed "Fujiyama," the sixteen-story residential building was the tallest in Pripyat, and its presence was the key element of her backup plan. She dashed through the dense wooded area between the abandoned shopping center and the broken hull of the communications center, sprinted across the street and dashed up the steps of Fujiyama.

She paused at the top step and looked back. Her instinct

for self-preservation told her to keep going, but she wanted to make sure the oborots followed her inside. She could not, if she could help it, leave this pack of beasts to potentially wreak havoc. Movement in the wooded area behind her told her they were coming. She fired off a shot in their direction to make sure they knew where she was, and then she dashed inside.

The interior was bare from years of looting, and she quickly found the stairs that would lead her up to the roof. She stopped at the doorway and waited for the oborots to appear. When the first one mounted the stairs, she fired off the last remaining shot in her clip and began her ascent.

By the time she reached the third floor landing, she wondered if she had made a mistake. Her legs burned and her breath came in gasps that echoed through the empty stairwell. She soldiered on, reminding herself of all the situations worse than this she'd come through, if not unscathed, then at least with life and limb intact. Over and over again, she picked her feet up and put them down, step after step flowing beneath her. The whole thing felt maddeningly like climbing up a down escalator. It was only the landings at each floor that proved to her that she was, indeed, making progress. She kept count, willing herself to keep moving.

Tenth floor…

Eleventh floor…

Twelfth floor…

As she mounted the steps at the thirteenth floor, the rotting wood gave way, and she went down hard. She could now hear the oborots clearly. They didn't seem to be gaining as rapidly as she would have expected, and she wondered if they had run into their own share of crumbling stairs. All of them were bigger and probably much heavier than her, so perhaps the stairs that had been strong enough to support her weight had not borne the burden of a pack of oborots so well. Anything that slowed them down was fine with her.

The final haul was sheer agony, every step a supreme effort

of will. She found herself grabbing onto the side rail to gain an extra boost. When she finally emerged on the roof, she had to fight off the urge to lie down and let the cool air wash over her.

*Almost there,* she told herself. *One more leg, and then the race is run.*

The door lay flat on the ground, so there was no hope of barring it and buying herself a little more time. She ran to the corner of the building, stripped off her pack, and dumped it out. What she needed now was at the bottom, and she hastily donned it before placing all the grenades in a row on the surface of the roof, stepped over the flimsy cable fence that ringed the top of Fujiyama, and turned back to face the doorway where the oborots would soon emerge. In the distance, the moonlight glistened on the surface of the sarcophagus that covered the Chernobyl reactor. In a different set of circumstances, she would find this place hauntingly beautiful, but now it was only a place of death to her.

When the oborots burst through the doorway, she started pulling pins and pitching grenades as fast as she could, careful to count down to the first detonation. The oborots did not spot her at first, but by the time she'd tossed the sixth grenade, an incendiary, they were coming for her. She pitched three more grenades, and as the first oborot leapt, she turned and hurled herself out into space.

The oborot shot past her, clawing the space she had occupied an instant before. The other oborots halted at the roof's edge, looked at her in confusion, and then the world exploded.

# CHAPTER 14

When she'd picked up her equipment from Deep Blue's contact, Queen's gut had told her to grab the wing suit, or "flying squirrel suit," on the remote chance that she found her way to the harbor barred. At the time, she had imagined it would be Manifold agents barring her way, not a pack of werewolf-like lab experiments gone wrong, but it had been a good call.

She spread her arms and sailed through the night, feeling the pressure of the air on the 'wings' below her arms and the 'tail' between her legs as she flew. Down below, the burning building behind her cast the city in a gold-tinged orange glow.

The suit wouldn't get her all the way to the harbor, but that didn't matter. It had gotten her away from the oborots and rendered pursuit impossible. She hoped her deadly mix of fragmentation and incendiary grenades had managed to get rid of the entire pack. Maybe the human beings they had once been did not deserve such a fate, but they were beyond redemption. At least they were no longer a threat to her or anyone else.

In the distance, the moon danced on the waters of the harbor as she glided past the town square. She kept her eyes peeled for the boat that would meet her, though she knew it would be running without lights. She hoped the fire atop Fujiyama would serve as a beacon drawing the craft closer to her.

The cool rush of air on her face invigorated her and renewed her sense of determination. She would report in to Deep Blue and then begin her search for Rook. And if Deep Blue had more orders for her, she'd use a Rookism and tell him to take a long walk on a short pier, though Rook would probably include a body part, rude gesture or something about farm animals.

As she neared the ground, she braced herself for a hard landing. Aiming for a thick stand of bushes, she released the parachute in her suit and felt the familiar yank as it slowed her descent. Her landing zone of choice softened the impact, but she still felt the jolt from toes to teeth. She crawled out of the brush to find herself in front of the Cinema Prometei, or the Prometheus Cinema. Years ago, a bronze statue of the Greek Titan had stood here until its removal in the late 1980's. Stripping out of her wing suit, she took one last look back at the city. Fire still glowed at the top of Fujiyama, a fitting backdrop for thoughts of the Titan who stole fire from Zeus.

The sound of a distant engine drew her attention back to the harbor. The silhouette of a small fishing boat appeared in the moonlight. Seeing her, the pilot brought the craft close to shore, and she waded out to meet it, aiming her pistol at his forehead, just in case.

"Who are you?" she demanded in Russian.

"Vladimir… I mean," the man cleared his throat, "I was told to say my name is Pawn."

"Who told you to say that?" She kept her weapon trained on him. He was an old man, his leathery skin deeply lined. His callused hands trembled as he held them above his head.

His eyes said two fears were doing battle inside of him: fear of Queen, and fear of what might happen to him if he answered her question truthfully. "You know I cannot tell you that."

"Good enough. Just don't try anything stupid and we'll be all right." She accepted his proffered hand, noting his strong grip, and let him haul her into the boat.

"Here are the things you asked for." He tossed her a canvas bag. Inside she found a change of clothes, along with boots, belt, another Mark 23 and holster, a knife and sheath, a bottle of water and some jerky.

"All right, Pawn, get us out of here, and no peeking while I change. I've gelded bigger men than you." She slid her KA-BAR from its sheath and stabbed it into the rail where she sat. The man gaped at it, and nodded his agreement. Queen grinned inwardly. She was not particularly modest, but she saw no harm in putting the fear of God, or rather, the fear of Queen, in his heart.

She stripped out of her clothing and tossed everything she'd worn into the water. The KA-BAR and Mark 23 she had used in the city followed. Spending a few hours in Pripyat would not expose one to a lethal dose of radiation, but prolonged exposure to contaminants that were stuck to clothing or weaponry was more dangerous.

When she was once again clothed, she sat staring out at the night sky as Vladimir guided their craft out into the Pripyat River. The first hint of dawn was on the horizon, and she picked up a photograph of a big man with intense blue eyes, dirty blonde hair, a long goatee and a mischievous smile. She'd held on to the picture when she ditched her clothes. She had brought it to show people as she conducted her search. At least, that's what she told herself. Now that she'd carried it into Pripyat, though, she'd have to toss it—after one last look.

"Is he a friend of yours?" Vladimir's voice interrupted her thoughts, and she turned angry eyes upon him. "I do not mean to intrude. I was just surprised because I saw that man not long ago."

In a flash, she had him by the collar and pulled him down so that they stood nose-to-nose. "What did you say?" She enunciated each word.

"I saw that man not long ago." Vladimir hurried on with

his explanation. "I was visiting some old friends, men I served with in the Military Maritime Fleet, and I saw him talking to a ship captain."

"You are sure you saw *this* man?" Queen thrust the picture in his face. "If you are the least bit uncertain, tell me now."

Vladimir took the picture in unsteady hands and stared at it for the span of five heartbeats before he nodded. He looked her square in the eye, his body trembling but his voice steady. "It was the same man. I am certain." Queen arched an eyebrow. "You do not forget a man like this. He is not, how do you say, a common specimen."

Queen snatched the picture away from him and tucked it into her pocket. She wanted desperately to believe Vladimir, but what if it was a mistake or a lie? "How is it that you overheard their conversation? My friend is very private about his business."

A moment of suspicion cross the sailor's face, but a quick reassessment of the situation told him he better tell Queen what he knew. "My friends work at the docks. I was wandering, waiting for them to finish some business. Your friend was speaking to a the captain, who I recognized as a competitor of my friends. Information can be a valuable commodity, one my friends sometimes pay for, so I wandered closer, hoping to overhear their conversation." He shrugged. "I managed to hear only a little bit before I sensed your friend watching me and decided to slip away."

"Tell me everything you heard." Queen's heart was racing. Finally, after the events of this horrific night, things just might be turning in her favor. *Nothing like a little dumb luck.* Vladimir told her all he could recall. It was not much. An injured Rook had been rescued and tended to by the sister of the sailor from whom he sought passage out of Russia. But Vladimir didn't know where they went.

"Tell you what, Vladimir, if your lead pans out, I'll see to it that you're rewarded. Now, tell me who this captain is and where I can find him."

The man's features relaxed. Clearly he had feared her reaction should she not believe him. "In Severodvinsk, in Russia. The ship is the *Songbird*, and the sailor's name is Maksim Dashkov."

Smiling a genuine smile for the first time in...she didn't know how long, Queen stretched out in the bottom of the boat and breathed deeply of the cool morning air. Exhausted as she was from her ordeal, her mind was racing. She was going to find Rook. She knew it.

# EPILOGUE

Darius rolled over and groaned. He put his hand to the side of his head and felt a ragged hole where his ear had been. He snatched his hand away, his fingers coming back bloody.

"Who the hell does that bitch think she is? Mike Tyson?" The words came out in wheezy rasp, and he rubbed his aching throat. She had almost been the death of him. He wondered why she had not taken the time to kill him. That was a big mistake on her part.

He hauled himself to his feet, feeling every bump and bruise he had sustained during the fight with the little, blonde Tasmanian devil. His eyes burned from the smoke and dust that hung in the air. He rubbed them with the back of his arm, but that only made it worse.

He took a deep breath and gagged on the acrid smoke that hung in the air. He would make an inspection, but he already knew what he'd find.

Five minutes later he was climbing out the emergency exit, his head wrapped in a blood-soaked bandage. He carried nothing with him. The girl had done a number on his facility, blowing up or burning all the offices and the laboratory. Nothing remained that was worth saving. He'd found all the holding pens empty, their doors wide open. He wondered why she had released them, and hoped they'd torn her to bits for her trouble.

Outside, dawn was breaking. Sirens wailed somewhere in the distance, warning him that his time was short. He turned to make for the river when a bright light caught his eye. He looked up to see that Fujiyama was on fire. He couldn't begin to fathom how or why she had done that.

He took off at a steady run, each step sending jolts of pain through his battered body. While he occasionally entertained thoughts of avenging his defeat at the hands of that...*woman*, she had unknowingly given him the keys to the magic kingdom. If Richard Ridley was dead, the throne could be claimed by its rightful heir, and there was only one man on the planet who could make such a claim:

Darius Ridley.

### FROM THE AUTHORS

We hope you enjoyed reading Callsign: Queen as much as we enjoyed writing it. Pripyat is a real and fascinating place, and the locations about which we have written are real. We did make one change for the sake of the story—Fujiyama is not located next to the town square. It's actually located on the western edge of town, and a different, not so well-known building stands in the spot where we've placed Fujiyama. Fujiyama is a well-known site in Pripyat and it would have been a shame to leave it out. Thanks for reading!

# ABOUT THE AUTHORS

**JEREMY ROBINSON** is the author of eleven novels including PULSE, INSTINCT, and THRESHOLD the first three books in his exciting Jack Sigler series. His novels have been translated into ten languages. He lives in New Hampshire with his wife and three children.

Visit him on the web, here:
www.jeremyrobinsononline.com

**DAVID WOOD** is the author of the Dane Maddock Adventures series, the historical adventure INTO THE WOODS, and the young adult thriller THE ZOMBIE-DRIVEN LIFE. Writing as David Debord, he is the author of the Absent Gods fantasy series. When not writing, David co-hosts ThrillerCast, a podcast dedicated to books and writing in the thriller genre.

Visit him on the web, here:
www.davidwoodweb.com

# COMING IN 2011

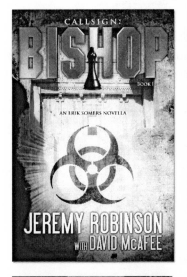

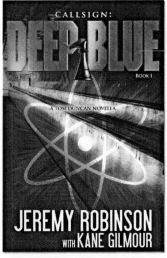

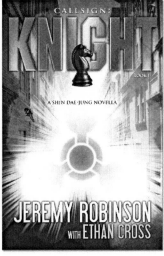

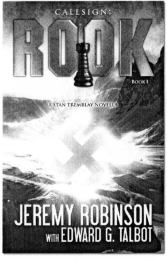

CPSIA information can be obtained at www.ICGtesting.com
Printed in the USA
BVOW05s1550030316

438763BV00001B/3/P